Addition Practice

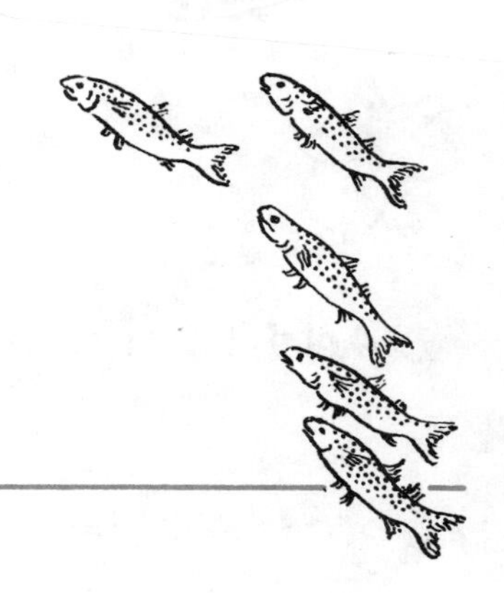

$$\begin{array}{rl} 4 & \text{addend} \\ +5 & \text{addend} \\ \hline 9 & \text{sum} \end{array}$$

Add to find the sums.

A.	3 +1	2 +5	4 +4	1 +6	7 +2
B.	4 +2	0 +9	6 +6	7 +3	3 +9
C.	9 +6	7 +7	4 +9	6 +2	7 +4
D.	5 +5	9 +8	8 +7	9 +9	8 +5
E.	9 +2	4 +8	8 +6	7 +6	9 +7

Skill: finding and writing sums

More Addition

Add to find the sums.

A.	6 + 5 = ____	7 + 3 = ____	3 + 5 = ____
B.	4 + 8 = ____	1 + 9 = ____	0 + 5 = ____
C.	1 + 3 = ____	5 + 7 = ____	3 + 6 = ____
D.	4 + 3 = ____	8 + 1 = ____	3 + 3 = ____
E.	4 + 9 = ____	6 + 6 = ____	5 + 3 = ____
F.	2 + 7 = ____	7 + 4 = ____	6 + 8 = ____
G.	2 + 8 = ____	0 + 7 = ____	8 + 4 = ____
H.	9 + 8 = ____	7 + 7 = ____	8 + 7 = ____
I.	3 + 8 = ____	7 + 9 = ____	9 + 4 = ____

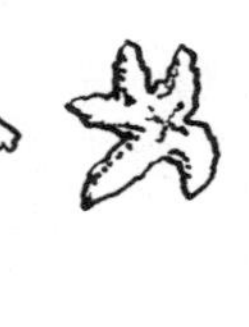

Skill: finding and writing sums

A number problem is hidden in each row. Draw a circle around the problems and put in the + and = signs.

1	2	8	3	+	4	=	7	6	9
6	1	7	4		5		8	4	3
3	3	9	5		2		5	6	11
2	5	4	9		3		6	8	1
9	7	5	3		6		2	8	9
4	3	5	5		10		8	4	11
6	3	4	2		5		7	8	3

Addition Squares

Add the numbers across and down. The last row down and the bottom row across will have the same answer.

2	2	4
3	4	7
5	6	11

A.

3	2	
1	4	

B.

1	4	
3	1	

C.

3	1	
1	3	

D.

5	1	
1	4	

E.

1	2	
3	4	

F.

3	3	
1	2	

G.

5	2	
2	5	

H.

3	5	
2	2	

Skill: using addition to find the missing numbers

Something's Missing!

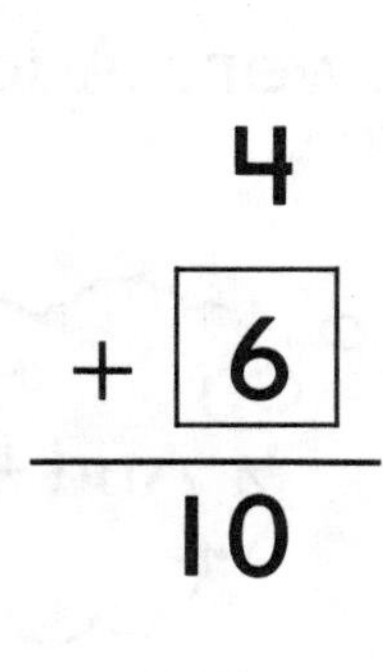

Find the missing addends.

A.

4	□	□	8	5
+ □	+ 2	+ 5	+ □	+ □
7	9	8	10	9

B.

8	6	□	9	□
+ □	+ □	+ 7	+ □	+ 6
11	12	10	17	15

C.

□	8	9	□	□
+ 7	+ □	+ □	+ 8	+ 9
13	16	14	12	18

Adding Three Numbers

Add the top two numbers. Find the answer. Add the bottom number to the answer.

Add.

A.	8	1	3	7	6	5
	1	5	4	2	3	4
	+ 9	+7	+8	+3	+7	+2
	18					

B.	1	4	9	2	3	4
	0	5	0	6	3	4
	+8	+1	+8	+9	+8	+4

Find the missing addends.

C.	2	□	5	6	□	2
	3	1	□	2	1	□
	+ 4	+ 6	+ 9	+ □	+ 4	+ 5
	9	8	18	15	12	15

Skills: adding three numbers; finding the missing addends

Subtraction Practice

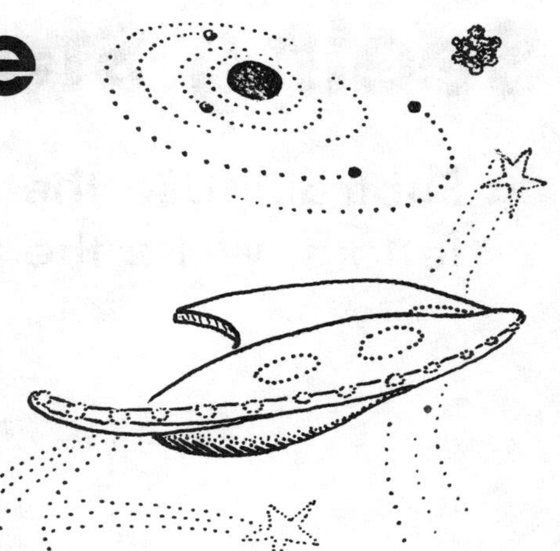

When you subtract, the answer you get is called the DIFFERENCE.

Subtract. Write the difference.

A. $8 - 4 =$ ____ $11 - 8 =$ ____ $6 - 6 =$ ____

B. $\begin{array}{r} 10 \\ -\ 9 \\ \hline \end{array}$ $\begin{array}{r} 12 \\ -\ 8 \\ \hline \end{array}$ $\begin{array}{r} 9 \\ -\ 3 \\ \hline \end{array}$ $\begin{array}{r} 13 \\ -\ 4 \\ \hline \end{array}$ $\begin{array}{r} 14 \\ -\ 7 \\ \hline \end{array}$

C. $13 - 7 =$ ____ $10 - 5 =$ ____ $12 - 3 =$ ____

D. $\begin{array}{r} 11 \\ -\ 5 \\ \hline \end{array}$ $\begin{array}{r} 14 \\ -\ 6 \\ \hline \end{array}$ $\begin{array}{r} 16 \\ -\ 9 \\ \hline \end{array}$ $\begin{array}{r} 10 \\ -\ 7 \\ \hline \end{array}$ $\begin{array}{r} 18 \\ -\ 9 \\ \hline \end{array}$

E. $12 - 7 =$ ____ $16 - 8 =$ ____ $14 - 5 =$ ____

F. $\begin{array}{r} 13 \\ -\ 9 \\ \hline \end{array}$ $\begin{array}{r} 15 \\ -\ 8 \\ \hline \end{array}$ $\begin{array}{r} 17 \\ -\ 9 \\ \hline \end{array}$ $\begin{array}{r} 11 \\ -\ 7 \\ \hline \end{array}$ $\begin{array}{r} 14 \\ -\ 8 \\ \hline \end{array}$

Skill: subtracting to find the difference

Seeing Stars

Subtract. Use the code. Match your answers with the letters. Write the letters in the boxes.

A.

8 − 7	13 − 9	12 − 5	14 − 6
1			
W			

B.

12 − 6	10 − 8		9 − 4

C.

14 − 7	6 − 6	14 − 9	11 − 8

code:

0	T
1	W
2	N
3	R
4	I
5	A
6	O
7	S
8	H

Skill: using subtraction to complete a code

Find the differences. Color the spaces with the answers:

2- red
3- green
4- white
5- purple
6- yellow
7- brown
8- blue
9- orange

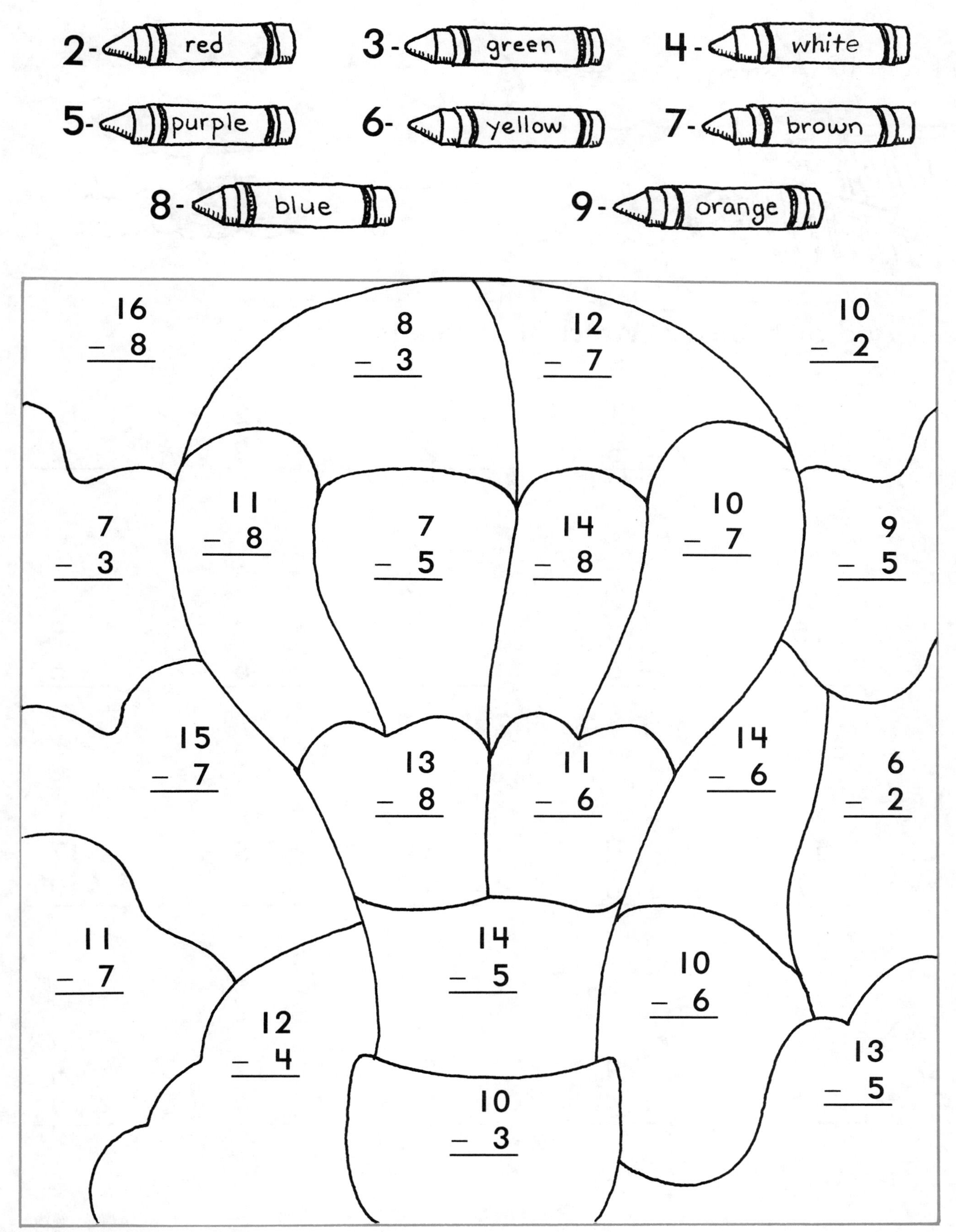

Skill: using subtraction to complete a picture

Addition and Subtraction Practice

Add or subtract. Watch the signs!

A.

$$\begin{array}{r} 7 \\ +\ 7 \\ \hline \end{array} \quad \begin{array}{r} 11 \\ -\ 5 \\ \hline \end{array} \quad \begin{array}{r} 9 \\ +\ 2 \\ \hline \end{array} \quad \begin{array}{r} 12 \\ -\ 3 \\ \hline \end{array} \quad \begin{array}{r} 10 \\ -\ 2 \\ \hline \end{array}$$

B.

$$\begin{array}{r} 15 \\ -\ 8 \\ \hline \end{array} \quad \begin{array}{r} 13 \\ -\ 6 \\ \hline \end{array} \quad \begin{array}{r} 9 \\ +\ 9 \\ \hline \end{array} \quad \begin{array}{r} 5 \\ +\ 6 \\ \hline \end{array} \quad \begin{array}{r} 9 \\ -\ 6 \\ \hline \end{array}$$

C.

$$\begin{array}{r} 12 \\ -\ 7 \\ \hline \end{array} \quad \begin{array}{r} 4 \\ +\ 6 \\ \hline \end{array} \quad \begin{array}{r} 15 \\ -\ 9 \\ \hline \end{array} \quad \begin{array}{r} 8 \\ +\ 7 \\ \hline \end{array} \quad \begin{array}{r} 17 \\ -\ 8 \\ \hline \end{array}$$

D.

$$\begin{array}{r} 7 \\ +\ 9 \\ \hline \end{array} \quad \begin{array}{r} 14 \\ -\ 6 \\ \hline \end{array} \quad \begin{array}{r} 5 \\ +\ 7 \\ \hline \end{array} \quad \begin{array}{r} 12 \\ -\ 9 \\ \hline \end{array} \quad \begin{array}{r} 4 \\ +\ 9 \\ \hline \end{array}$$

Skill: practicing addition and subtraction skills

Add or subtract.

A. 5 + 3 = ____ 9 − 2 = ____ 4 + 6 = ____

B. 7 + 9 = ____ 5 + 8 = ____ 13 − 7 = ____

C. 11 − 9 = ____ 17 − 9 = ____ 7 + 4 = ____

D. 12 − 3 = ____ 9 + 4 = ____ 8 + 9 = ____

E. 14 − 8 = ____ 15 − 7 = ____ 8 + 7 = ____

Try these:

F. 5 ☐ 1 = 6 8 ☐ 2 = 6

G. 4 ☐ 5 = 9 7 ☐ 3 = 4

Adding Tens and Ones

Add the ones. Then add the tens.

A.

tens	ones
2	0
+2	4
4	4

tens	ones
4	6
+	3

tens	ones
4	5
+5	2

tens	ones
3	4
+4	4

B.

$$\begin{array}{r} 6 \\ +\ 12 \\ \hline \end{array} \qquad \begin{array}{r} 18 \\ +\ 30 \\ \hline \end{array} \qquad \begin{array}{r} 33 \\ +\ 21 \\ \hline \end{array} \qquad \begin{array}{r} 7 \\ +\ 42 \\ \hline \end{array}$$

C.

$$\begin{array}{r} 58 \\ +\ 1 \\ \hline \end{array} \qquad \begin{array}{r} 63 \\ +\ 26 \\ \hline \end{array} \qquad \begin{array}{r} 40 \\ +\ 12 \\ \hline \end{array} \qquad \begin{array}{r} 23 \\ +\ 43 \\ \hline \end{array}$$

Add the ones.
Then add the tens.

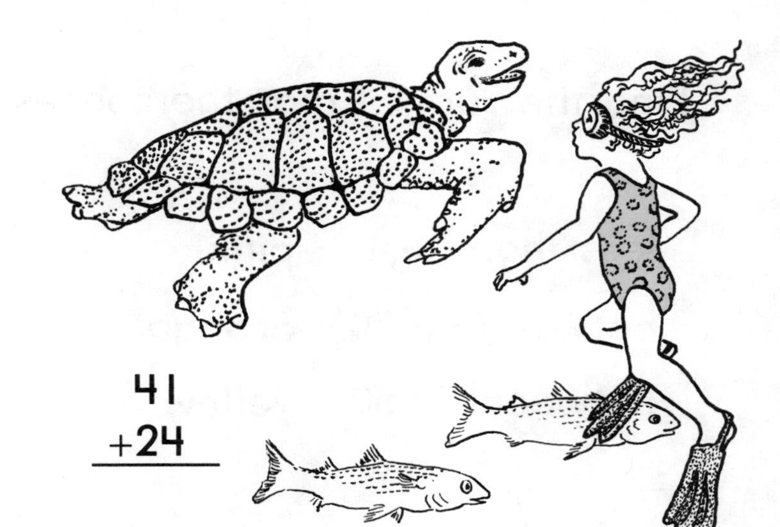

A.

52	36	41
+12	+13	+24

B.

73	25	33	16	90
+13	+52	+25	+53	+ 4

C.

19	42	40	34	12
+80	+36	+53	+34	+43

D.

57	32	83	32	26
+21	+54	+14	+16	+33

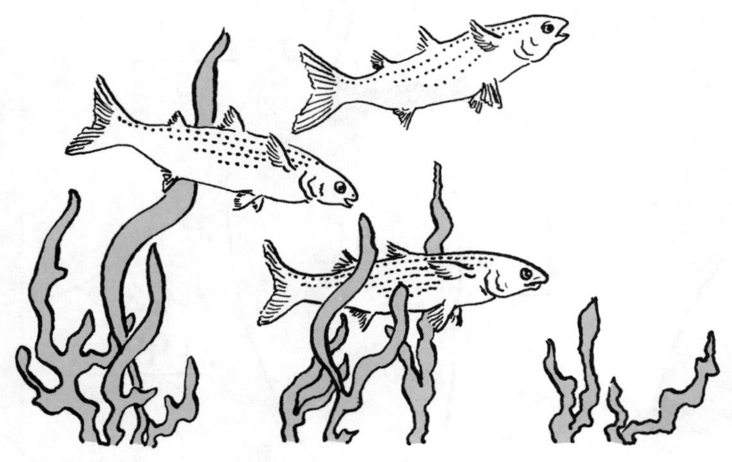

E.

43	95
+22	+ 4

Skill: adding tens and ones

Find the sums. Color the spaces with the answers:

less than 40	pink	between 60-70	green
between 40-50	orange	between 70-80	blue
between 50-60	yellow	greater than 80	red

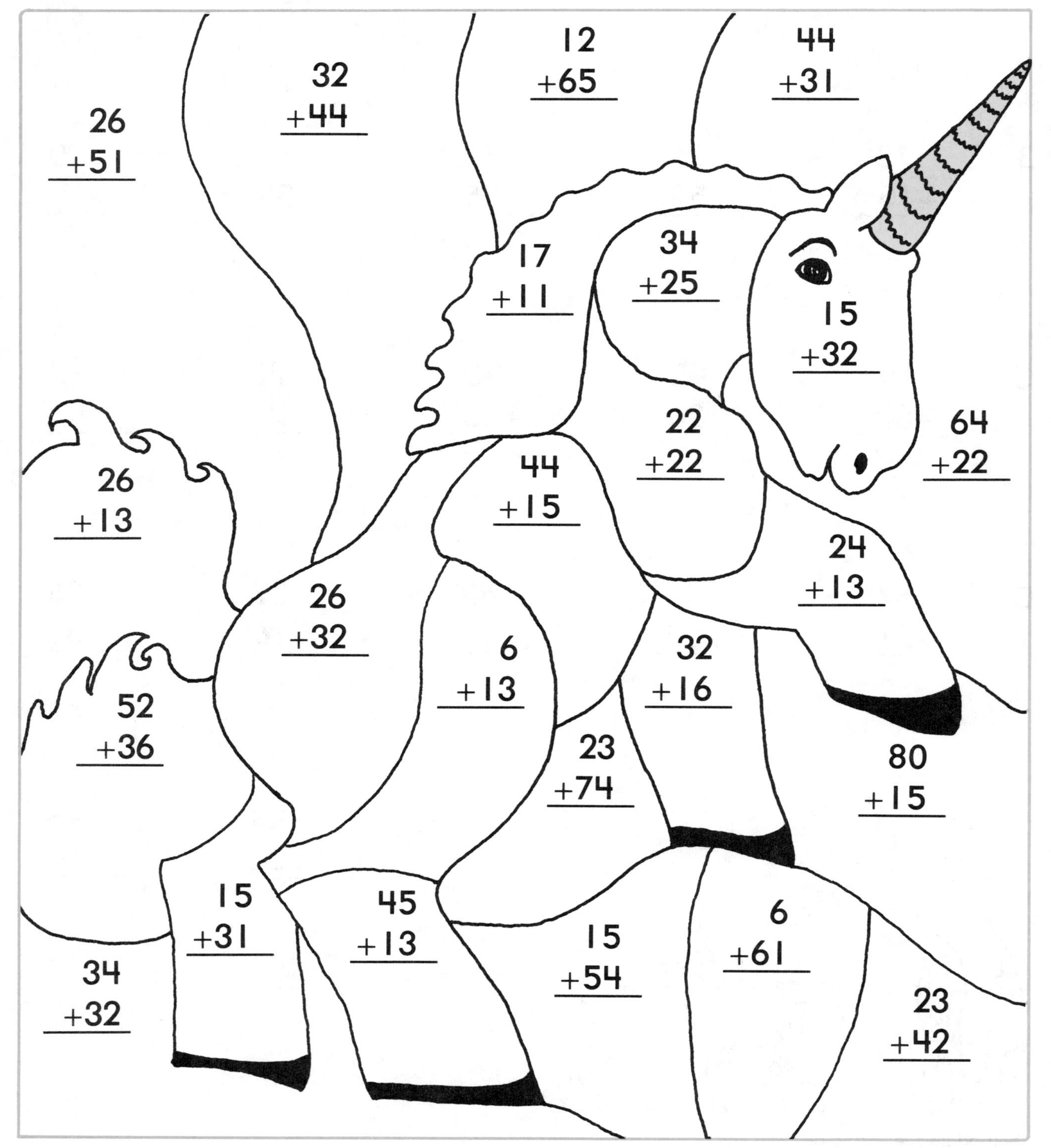

Skill: using addition to complete a hidden picture

More Column Addition

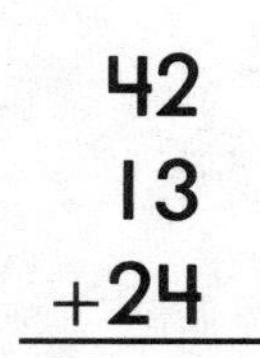

```
  42
  13
+24
----
```

tens	ones
4	2
1	3
+2	4
	9

tens	ones
4	2
1	3
+2	4
7	9

Add the ones. Then add the tens.

A.

```
  32      51      43      60
  56      24      31      14
+11     +23     +13     +23
----    ----    ----    ----
```

B.

```
  22      61      35      21
  24      15      22      22
+12     + 3     +32     +20
----    ----    ----    ----
```

Find the missing addends.

C.

```
  6[2]     4 2     [ ]1     7 0
  2 4     [ ]6     2 2     1[ ]
[+1]3    +1[ ]    +2[ ]    [+ ]6
-----    -----    -----    -----
  9 9      8 9     7 8      9 7
```

Subtracting Tens and Ones

tens	ones
4	8
−2	3
	5

tens	ones
4	8
−2	3
2	5

Subtract the ones. Then subtract the tens.

A.

tens	ones
3	5
−1	3
2	2

tens	ones
6	7
−2	6

tens	ones
2	7
−	3

tens	ones
5	8
−4	6

B.

$$\begin{array}{r} 88 \\ -\ 52 \\ \hline \end{array} \qquad \begin{array}{r} 25 \\ -\ 12 \\ \hline \end{array} \qquad \begin{array}{r} 59 \\ -\ 26 \\ \hline \end{array} \qquad \begin{array}{r} 82 \\ -\ 12 \\ \hline \end{array}$$

C.

$$\begin{array}{r} 68 \\ -\ 51 \\ \hline \end{array} \qquad \begin{array}{r} 74 \\ -\ 32 \\ \hline \end{array} \qquad \begin{array}{r} 57 \\ -\ 42 \\ \hline \end{array} \qquad \begin{array}{r} 29 \\ -\ 16 \\ \hline \end{array}$$

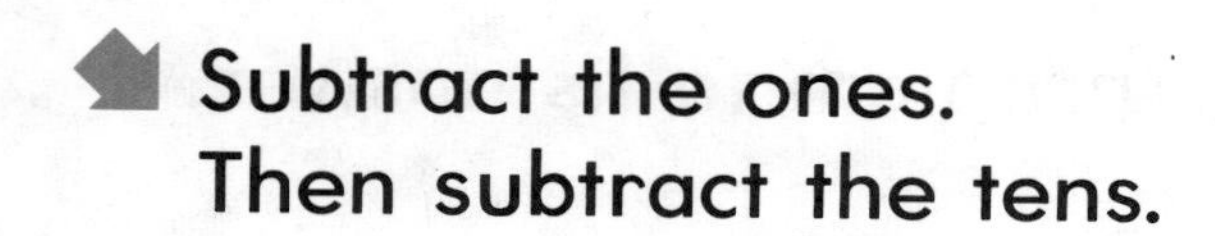
Subtract the ones.
Then subtract the tens.

A.	57 −12	48 −24	36 −25		
B.	66 −36	96 −55	38 −16	98 −63	82 −41
C.	75 −25	86 −24	65 −41	77 −64	66 −35
D.	87 −35	68 −32	94 −30	84 −21	79 −24
E.				94 −62	78 −32

Skill: subtracting tens and ones

Subtract. Draw a line from the problem to its answer.

Skill: subtracting two-digit numbers

Add or subtract.

A.	26 +12 38	78 −25	45 +44	59 −11	11 +77
B.	36 − 2	42 +25	85 −23	23 +26	99 −76
C.	46 +20	48 −15	31 +26	97 −33	43 +25

Skill: adding and subtracting two-digit numbers without regrouping

More Practice

Add or subtract. Watch the signs.

A.	75 −13	21 +47	42 +15	59 −37	82 +16
B.	33 +13	65 −25	18 +60	24 +42	96 −91
C.	17 +22	75 +13	86 −33	46 −30	55 +34
D.	63 −32	18 +81	29 −19	44 +35	77 −52

Skill: adding and subtracting two-digit numbers without regrouping

Let's Regroup

Add.

$$\begin{array}{r} 37 \\ +45 \\ \hline \end{array}$$

Add the ones.

tens	ones
1	
3	7
+4	5
	2

Add the tens.

tens	ones
1	
3	7
+4	5
8	2

Add.

$$\begin{array}{r} 1 \\ 37 \\ +45 \\ \hline 82 \end{array}$$

Find the sums.

A.

tens	ones
1	
4	5
+3	9
8	4

tens	ones
2	6
+1	5

tens	ones
3	7
+4	8

tens	ones
1	2
+5	9

tens	ones
5	6
+2	7

B.

$\begin{array}{r} 84 \\ +\ 7 \\ \hline \end{array}$ $\begin{array}{r} 36 \\ +45 \\ \hline \end{array}$ $\begin{array}{r} 52 \\ +28 \\ \hline \end{array}$ $\begin{array}{r} 74 \\ +17 \\ \hline \end{array}$ $\begin{array}{r} 25 \\ +49 \\ \hline \end{array}$

C.

$\begin{array}{r} 8 \\ +35 \\ \hline \end{array}$ $\begin{array}{r} 17 \\ +45 \\ \hline \end{array}$ $\begin{array}{r} 53 \\ +38 \\ \hline \end{array}$ $\begin{array}{r} 55 \\ +28 \\ \hline \end{array}$ $\begin{array}{r} 78 \\ +16 \\ \hline \end{array}$

Skill: adding with regrouping (carrying)

Don't forget to regroup!

Add.

A.	1 19 +29 48	35 +59	25 +26	54 +16	
B.	5 +37	24 +19	57 +14	49 +12	8 +85
C.	35 +16	29 +43	22 +68	16 +36	47 +27
D.	46 +29	18 +58	36 +25	37 +37	79 +17

Skill: adding with regrouping (carrying)

Regrouping Practice

Add.

A.	$\begin{array}{r} ^{1}\\ 62 \\ +19 \\ \hline 81 \end{array}$	$\begin{array}{r} 73 \\ +\ 9 \\ \hline \end{array}$	$\begin{array}{r} 38 \\ +19 \\ \hline \end{array}$	$\begin{array}{r} 27 \\ +36 \\ \hline \end{array}$	$\begin{array}{r} 27 \\ +48 \\ \hline \end{array}$
B.	$\begin{array}{r} 35 \\ +\ 9 \\ \hline \end{array}$	$\begin{array}{r} 81 \\ +\ 9 \\ \hline \end{array}$	$\begin{array}{r} 55 \\ +28 \\ \hline \end{array}$	$\begin{array}{r} 64 \\ +29 \\ \hline \end{array}$	$\begin{array}{r} 47 \\ +39 \\ \hline \end{array}$
C.	$\begin{array}{r} 16 \\ +19 \\ \hline \end{array}$	$\begin{array}{r} 56 \\ +14 \\ \hline \end{array}$	$\begin{array}{r} 47 \\ +25 \\ \hline \end{array}$	$\begin{array}{r} 29 \\ +26 \\ \hline \end{array}$	$\begin{array}{r} 45 \\ +35 \\ \hline \end{array}$
D.	$\begin{array}{r} 29 \\ +37 \\ \hline \end{array}$	$\begin{array}{r} 48 \\ +12 \\ \hline \end{array}$	$\begin{array}{r} 66 \\ +16 \\ \hline \end{array}$	$\begin{array}{r} 55 \\ +39 \\ \hline \end{array}$	$\begin{array}{r} 18 \\ +63 \\ \hline \end{array}$

Regrouping with Subtraction

When you cannot subtract the bottom number from the top number, this is what you must do:

Subtract.

$$\begin{array}{r} 45 \\ -17 \\ \hline \end{array}$$

Regroup.

tens	ones
3	15
~~4~~	~~5~~
−1	7

In subtraction, regrouping means to borrow.

Subtract the ones first.

tens	ones
3	15
~~4~~	~~5~~
−1	7
	8

Subtract the tens, next.

tens	ones
3	15
~~4~~	~~5~~
−1	7
2	8

Practice.

A.

tens	ones
3	18
~~4~~	~~8~~
−	9
3	9

tens	ones
3	2
−1	7

tens	ones
4	4
−3	7

tens	ones
7	2
−5	6

tens	ones
5	0
−3	5

B.

$$\begin{array}{r} 65 \\ -16 \\ \hline \end{array} \qquad \begin{array}{r} 52 \\ -27 \\ \hline \end{array} \qquad \begin{array}{r} 61 \\ -44 \\ \hline \end{array} \qquad \begin{array}{r} 84 \\ -26 \\ \hline \end{array} \qquad \begin{array}{r} 94 \\ -28 \\ \hline \end{array}$$

Skill: subtracting with regrouping (borrowing)

Regroup.
Subtract the ones.
Subtract the tens.

A.

tens	ones
7	12
~~8~~	~~2~~
−6	3
1	9

$$\begin{array}{r} 35 \\ -17 \\ \hline \end{array} \quad \begin{array}{r} 57 \\ -29 \\ \hline \end{array} \quad \begin{array}{r} 64 \\ -25 \\ \hline \end{array} \quad \begin{array}{r} 44 \\ -18 \\ \hline \end{array}$$

B.

$$\begin{array}{r} 61 \\ -49 \\ \hline \end{array} \quad \begin{array}{r} 73 \\ -18 \\ \hline \end{array} \quad \begin{array}{r} 81 \\ -36 \\ \hline \end{array} \quad \begin{array}{r} 98 \\ -19 \\ \hline \end{array} \quad \begin{array}{r} 52 \\ -27 \\ \hline \end{array}$$

C.

$$\begin{array}{r} 31 \\ -18 \\ \hline \end{array} \quad \begin{array}{r} 82 \\ -34 \\ \hline \end{array} \quad \begin{array}{r} 28 \\ -19 \\ \hline \end{array} \quad \begin{array}{r} 94 \\ -86 \\ \hline \end{array} \quad \begin{array}{r} 31 \\ -12 \\ \hline \end{array}$$

D.

$$\begin{array}{r} 34 \\ -16 \\ \hline \end{array} \quad \begin{array}{r} 65 \\ -57 \\ \hline \end{array} \quad \begin{array}{r} 42 \\ -26 \\ \hline \end{array} \quad \begin{array}{r} 57 \\ -18 \\ \hline \end{array} \quad \begin{array}{r} 93 \\ -45 \\ \hline \end{array}$$

E.

$$\begin{array}{r} 33 \\ -14 \\ \hline \end{array} \quad \begin{array}{r} 77 \\ -39 \\ \hline \end{array} \quad \begin{array}{r} 24 \\ -18 \\ \hline \end{array} \quad \begin{array}{r} 44 \\ -29 \\ \hline \end{array} \quad \begin{array}{r} 86 \\ -49 \\ \hline \end{array}$$

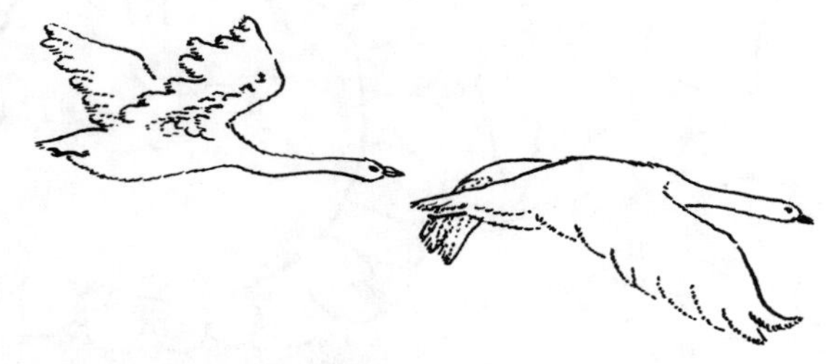

Regroup. Subtract.
Color the spaces with the answers:

red — differences greater than 27

blue — differences between 19 and 27

yellow — differences less than 19

62	61	53	84	34	90	55
−48	−27	−29	−76	−18	−53	−37

44	68	50	31	27	82	40
−16	−29	−27	−19	− 9	−53	−12

A Mixed-Up Rainbow!

Regroup. Subtract.
Color the spaces with the answers:

between 10-20	red	between 40-50	blue
between 20-30	orange	between 50-60	green
between 30-40	yellow	between 60-70	purple

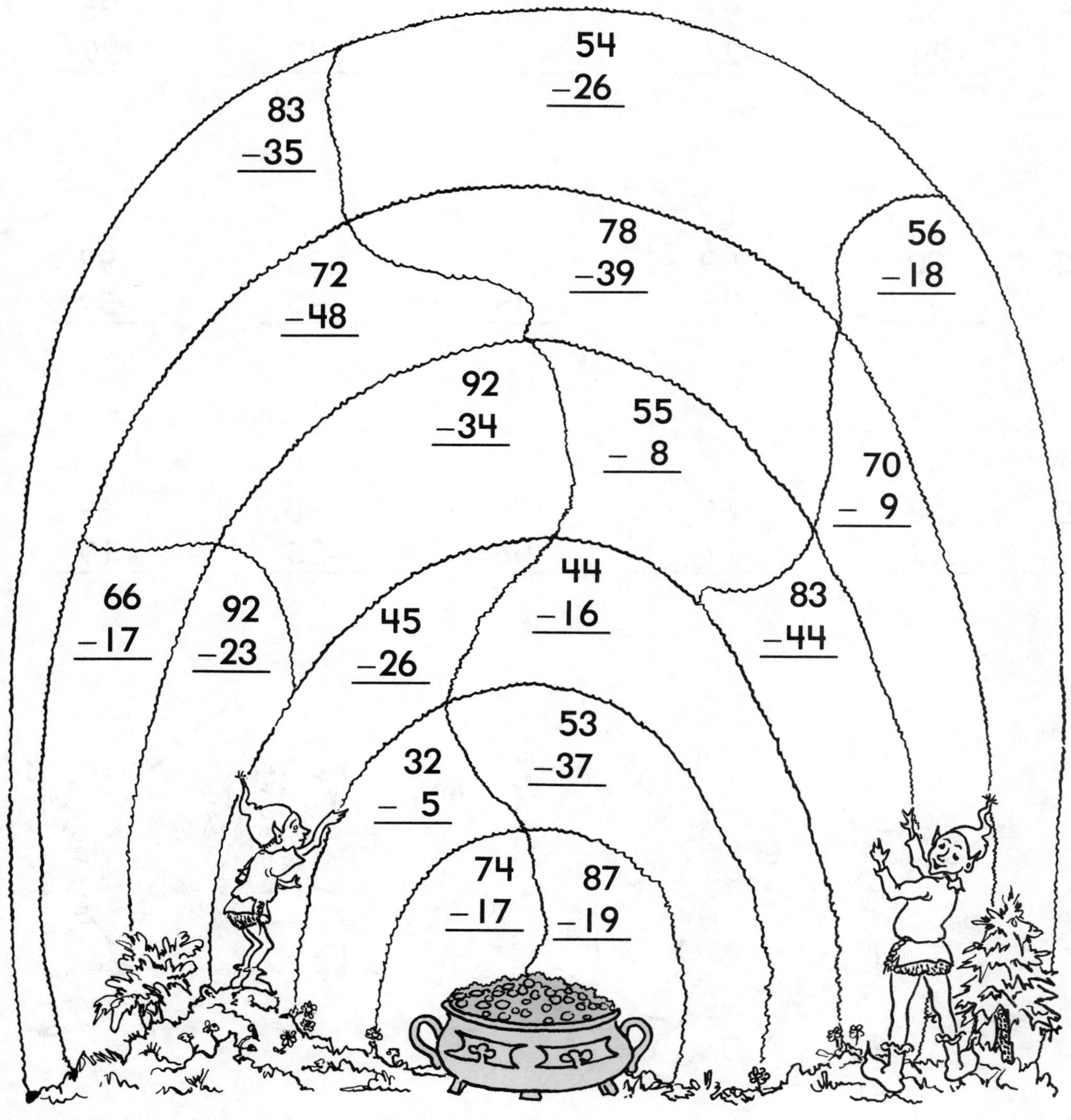

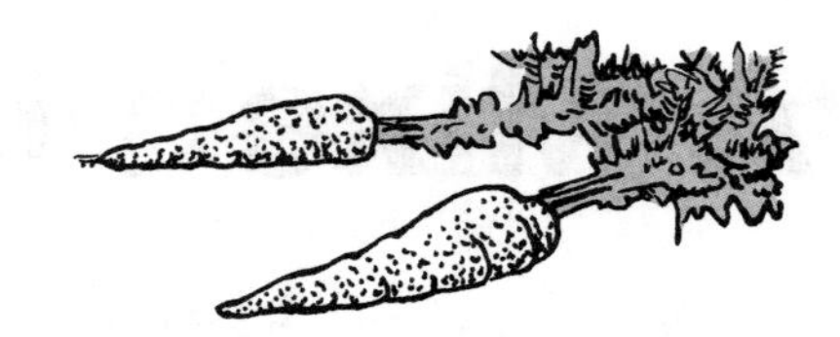

Regroup. Add or subtract.
Watch the signs!

A.	70 −23	59 +12	78 +17	42 −23	50 −47
B.	67 +24	91 −27	40 −27	39 +43	75 −29
C.	80 −48	49 +45	42 +38	73 −45	92 −59
D.	58 +17	69 +11	97 −48	60 −25	64 +19

Skill: adding and subtracting with regrouping

Regroup. Add or subtract. Match your answers to the number under each line. Write the letters from the answer boxes on the lines.

A	D	E	G	H
71 +19	75 −16	24 +36	93 −28	52 +19
I	**K**	**L**	**N**	**P**
45 −17	56 +27	78 −39	24 +27	62 −28
R	**S**	**T**	**U**	**Y**
92 −29	73 +18	72 −36	25 +56	56 −39

Why do elephants float on their backs?

T O
36

___ ___ ___ ___ ___ ___ ___ ___ ___
83 60 60 34 36 71 60 28 63

___ ___ ___ ___ ___ ___ ___ ___ ___ ___
91 81 51 65 39 90 91 91 60 91

___ ___ ___
59 63 17

Add or subtract. Then help the mouse go through the maze by connecting the answers in order.

A.	B.	C.	D.	E.	F.
90	24	72	50	62	94
− 8	+72	−28	− 7	+29	−17
82					

G.	H.	I.	J.	K.	L.
15	49	46	80	82	91
+75	+31	+46	− 9	−16	−18

M.	N.	O.	P.	Q.	R.
45	36	71	24	66	90
+25	+45	−29	+29	+35	−49

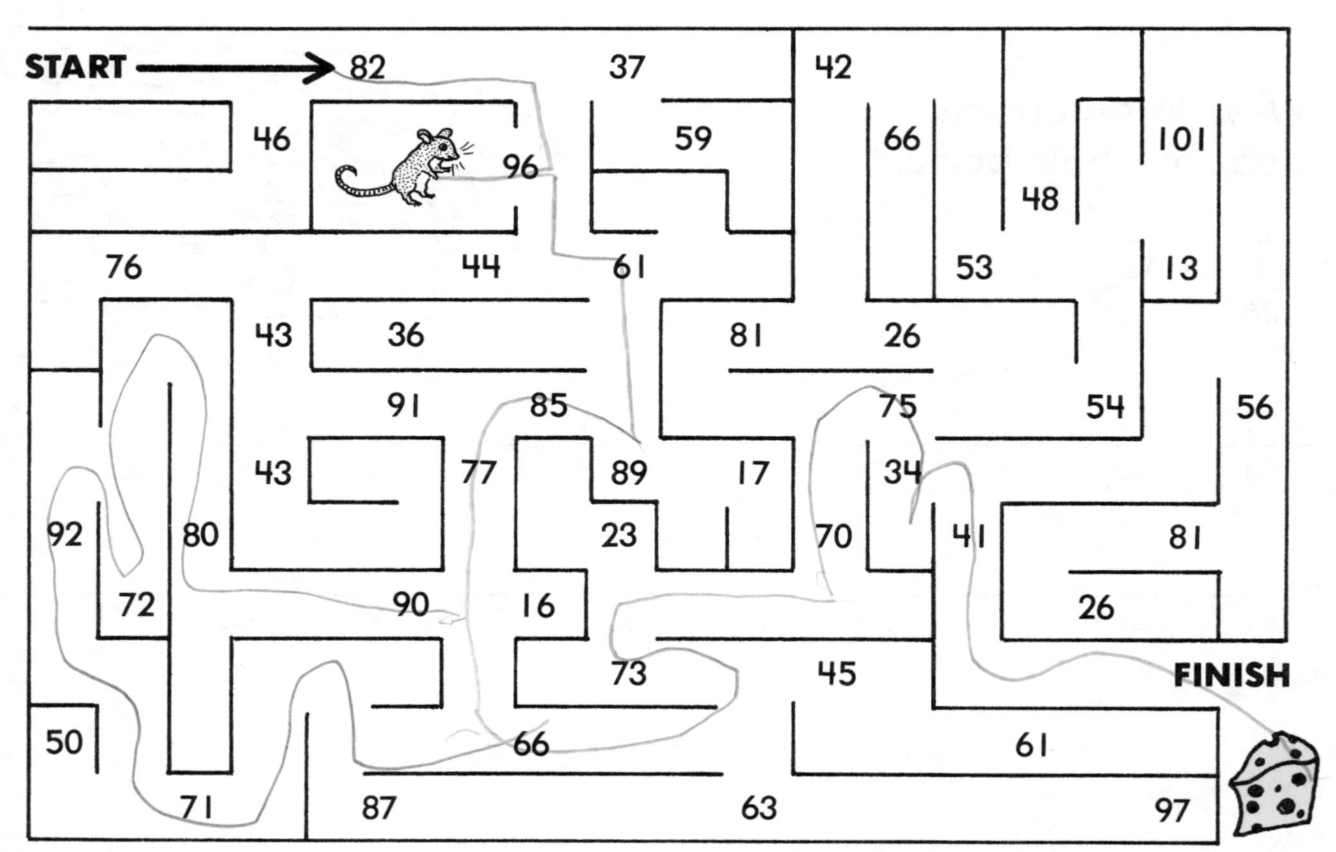

Skills: adding and subtracting two-digit numbers; solving a maze

Word Problems

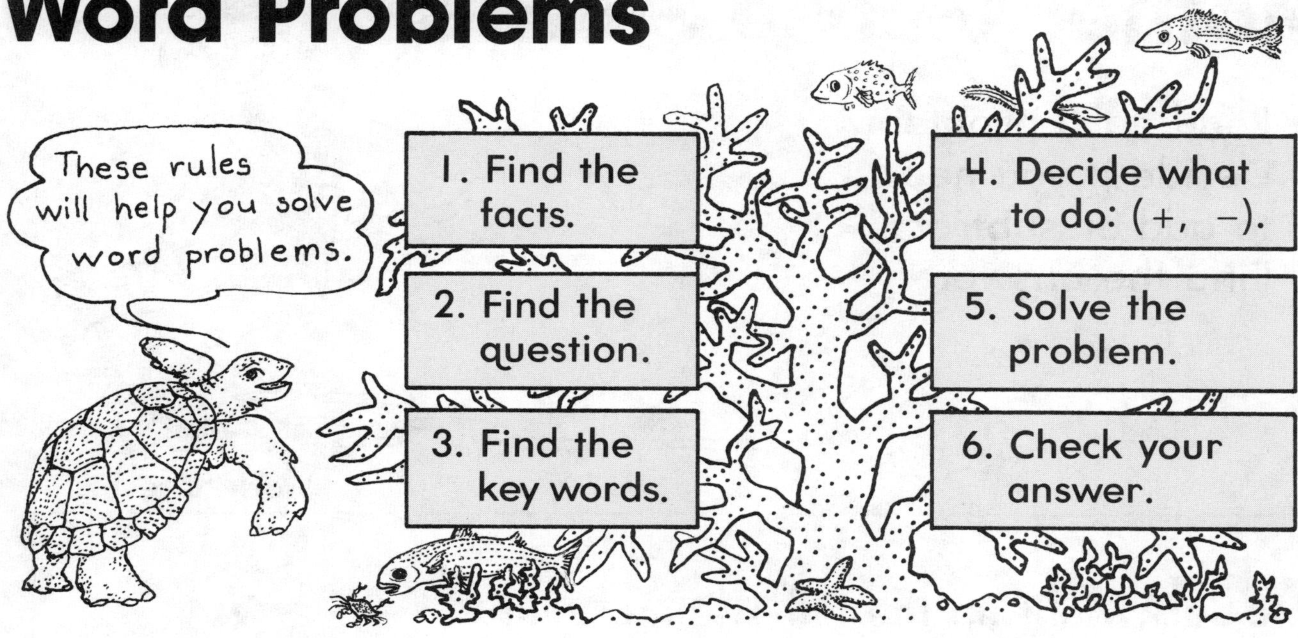

Read each problem. Decide if you need to add or subtract. Find the answer.

A. 7 girls came to Ann's birthday party. 8 boys came, too. How many children came to the party in all?

7 + 8 = ☐

B. Mother bought 8 red party hats and 9 blue party hats. How many party hats did Mother buy in all?

__________ = ☐

C. 9 children had chocolate ice cream. 7 children had cake. How many more children had ice cream than cake?

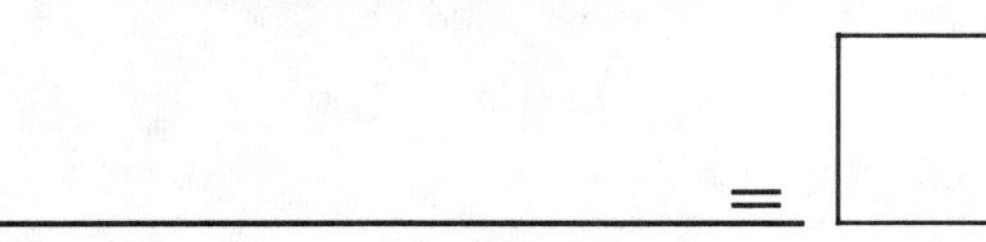

__________ = ☐

D. Father took 6 pictures. Mother took 9 pictures. How many more pictures did Mother take than Father?

__________ = ☐

E. Father blew up 5 red balloons, 3 yellow balloons, and 6 green balloons. How many balloons did he blow up in all?

__________ = ☐

F. 3 children walked home. 12 children went home in cars. How many more children went home in cars than walked home?

__________ = ☐

Mother Goose Stories

Read each problem.
Decide if you need
to add or subtract.
Find the answer.

	Work here.
A. Jack went up the hill 17 times. Jill went up the hill 34 times. How many more times did Jill go up the hill than Jack?	$\begin{array}{r} 34 \\ -17 \\ \hline \end{array}$
B. Peter Piper picked 25 pickled peppers on Monday. On Tuesday, he picked 34 more. How many pickled peppers did Peter Piper pick in all?	
C. The three little kittens lost 26 mittens in December. In January, they lost 25 more. How many mittens did they lose in all?	
D. Little Bo Peep had 53 sheep. One day she lost 18 of them. How many sheep did she have left?	

Skill: using addition and subtraction to solve word problems

Fit as a Fiddle

Read the table.

Fitness Fun Run

Laps	Girls	Boys
1 lap	34	26
2 laps	12	21
3 laps	27	34

Read each problem. Decide if you need to add or subtract. Find the answer.

	Work here.
A. 26 boys ran 1 lap. 34 girls ran 1 lap. How many more girls than boys ran 1 lap?	
B. 27 girls ran 3 laps. 34 boys ran 3 laps. How many boys and girls ran 3 laps?	
C. How many girls ran in all?	
D. How many boys ran in all?	
E. How many more boys ran than girls? (Hint: use your answers from 3 and 4.)	

Skill: using addition and subtraction to solve word problems

Hobby Day

Read each problem. Decide if you need to add or subtract. Find the answer.

Work here.

A. Josê brought his stamp collection. He has 38 American stamps and 57 stamps from other countries. How many stamps does he have in all?	
B. Marcia brought her shell collection. She has 43 shells that she found at the beach. She bought 21 shells at a shop. How many more shells did she find than buy?	
C. Bart and Brian collect baseball cards. Bart has 57 cards in his collection. Brian has 74 cards. How many more cards does Brian have than Bart?	
D. Lin collects pretty rocks. She found 26 rocks around her neighborhood. She found 29 rocks on vacations. How many rocks does Lin have in all?	

Skill: using addition and subtraction to solve word problems

Hundreds, Tens and Ones

How many hundreds, tens and ones?

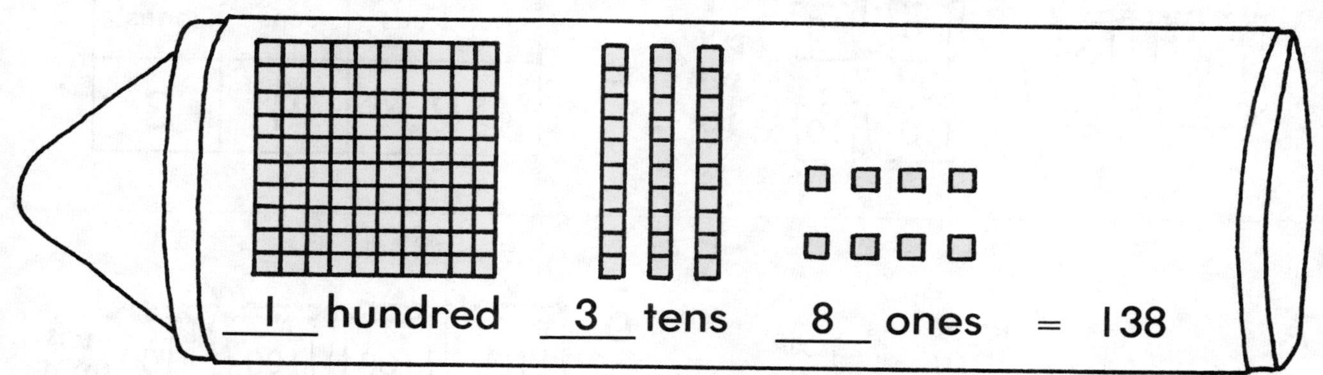

Write the numbers on the lines.

A.

3 hundreds 2 tens 6 ones = 326

5 hundreds 8 tens 4 ones = ______

6 hundreds 1 ten 5 ones = ______

B.

472 = ______ hundreds ______ tens ______ ones

926 = ______ hundreds ______ tens ______ ones

153 = ______ hundred ______ tens ______ ones

C.

4 hundreds 3 tens 8 ones = ______

6 hundreds 2 tens 0 ones = ______

3 hundreds 0 tens 5 ones = ______

D.

850 = ______ hundreds ______ tens ______ ones

407 = ______ hundreds ______ tens ______ ones

<u>Skill:</u> understanding hundreds, tens and ones

Count the hundreds, tens and ones. Write the numbers in the boxes.

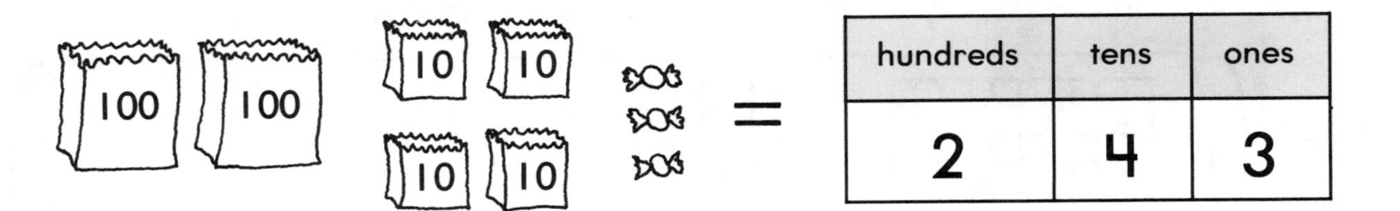

hundreds	tens	ones
2	4	3

A.

hundreds	tens	ones

B.

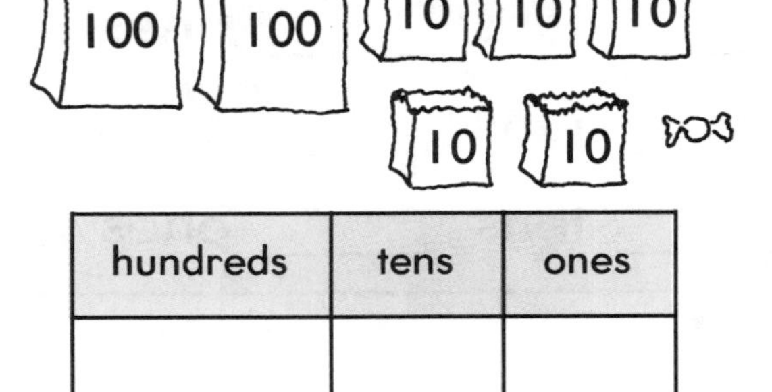

hundreds	tens	ones

C.

hundreds	tens	ones

D.

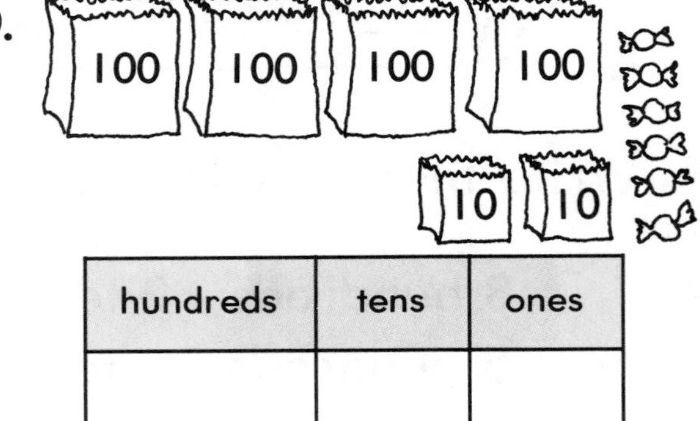

hundreds	tens	ones

E.

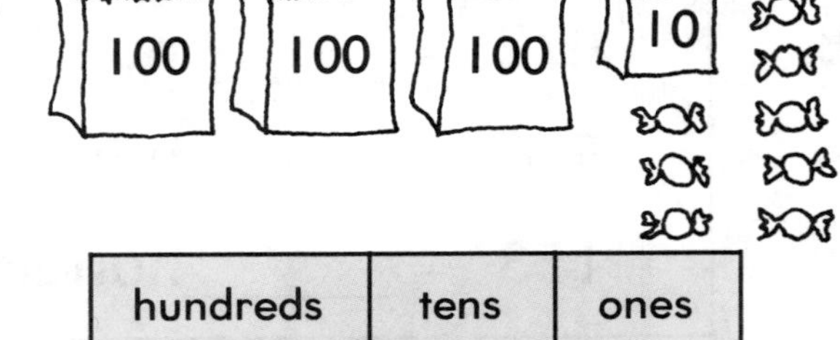

hundreds	tens	ones

F.

hundreds	tens	ones

Skill: writing hundreds, tens and ones

Dot to Dot

Start at 100.
Connect the dots in order.

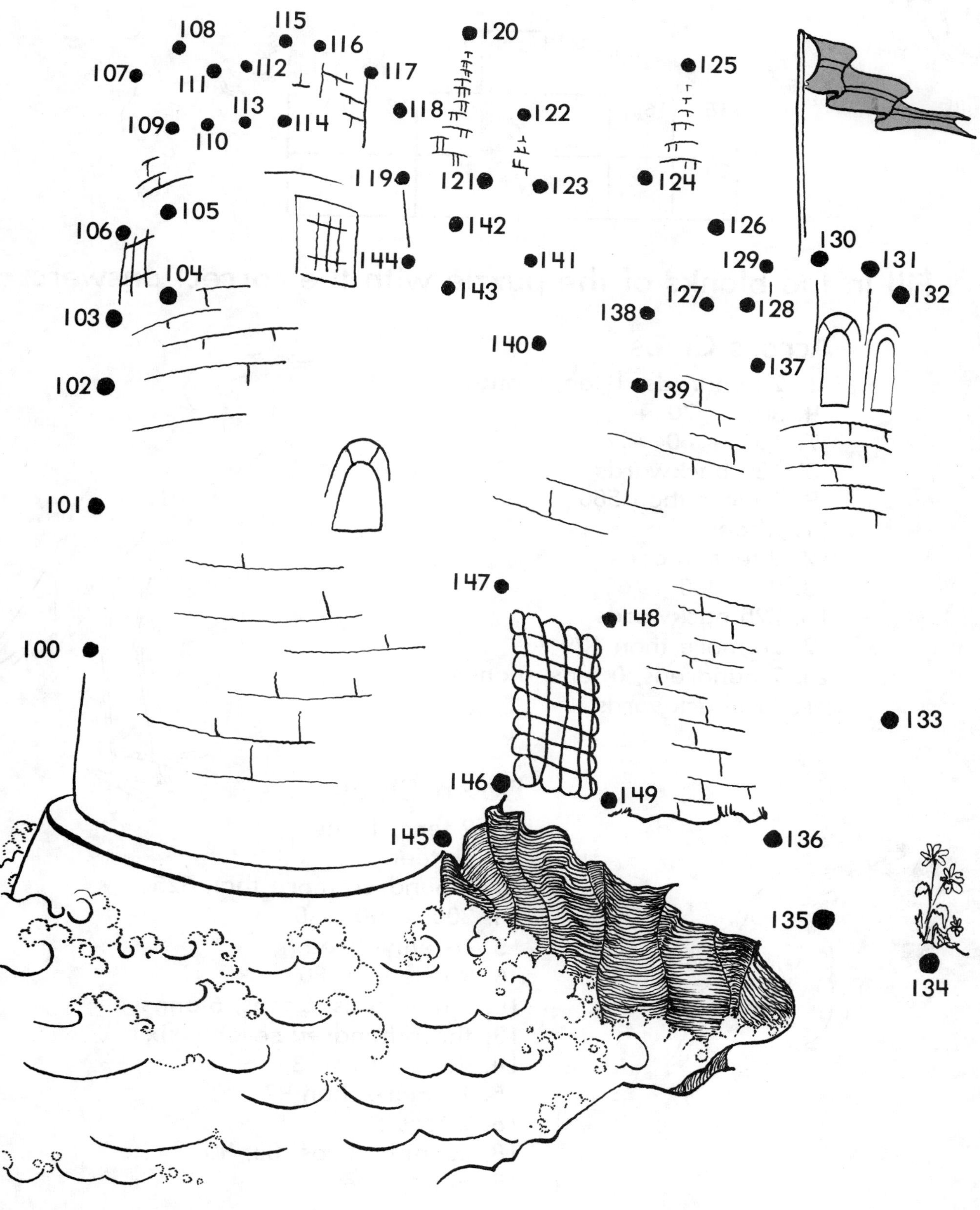

1	2	3		4	5	6
7				8		
		9	10			
11					12	
		13		14		
15	16			17	18	19
20				21		

Fill in the blanks of the puzzle with the correct answers.

Across Clues

1. 2 hundreds, 1 ten, 8 ones
4. 300 + 70 + 7
7. 100 + 60 + 2
8. 134 backwards
9. 10 less than 580
11. fifteen
12. 9 tens, 8 ones
13. 4 + 300 + 60
15. 725 backwards
17. 20 more than 129
20. 7 hundreds, 0 tens, 6 ones
21. 123 backwards

Down Clues

1. 2 tens, 1 one
2. sixteen
3. 2 hundred more than 625
4. 300 + 40 + 0
5. seventy-three
6. 9 less than 80
10. 7 hundreds, 6 tens, 6 ones
13. three hundred seventy-six
14. 400 + 10 + 3
15. 10 more than 47
16. 2 tens
18. count by twos: 38, 40, ?
19. ninety-one

Skill: understanding place value

Adding Hundreds, Tens and Ones

Add the ones.

hundreds	tens	ones
3	2	5
+1	6	2
		7

Add the tens.

hundreds	tens	ones
3	2	5
+1	6	2
	8	7

Add the hundreds.

hundreds	tens	ones
3	2	5
+ 1	6	2
4	8	7

Add.

A.	714 + 122	162 + 516	420 + 375	372 + 214
B.	307 + 252	437 + 361	687 + 212	404 + 243
C.	422 + 374	395 + 203	555 + 234	306 + 182
D.	362 + 217	514 + 153	413 + 151	348 + 201

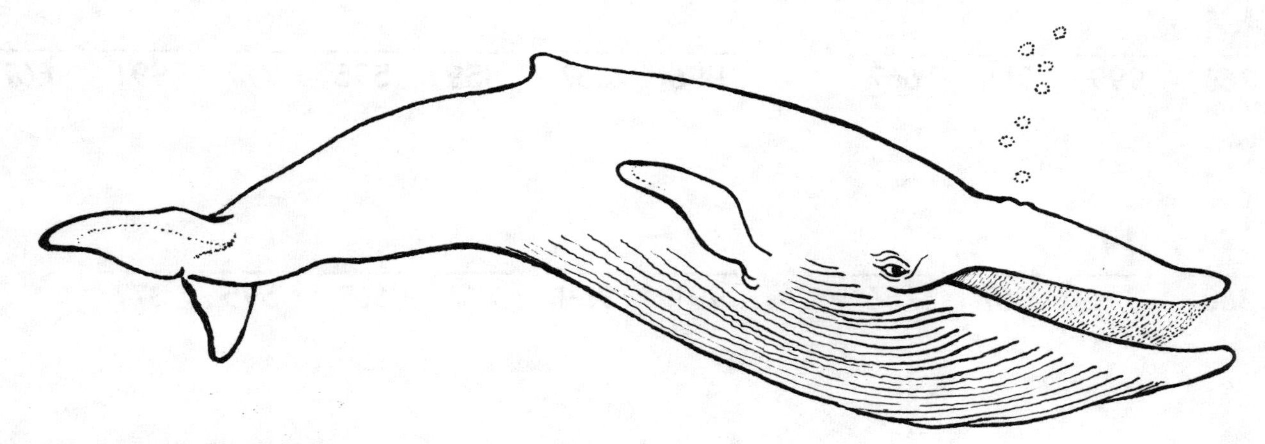

Skill: adding hundreds, tens and ones

Add. Match your answers to the number under each line. Write the letters from the answer boxes on the lines.

A 432 +163	B 174 +322	C 816 + 43	E 253 +414
I 519 +480	K 254 +123	M 425 +341	Q 803 +151
S 731 +260	T 345 + 23	U 624 +153	Y 235 +521

What animals sometimes need to be oiled?

M	___	___	___	,	___	___	___	___	___	___	___
766	999	859	667		496	667	859	595	777	991	667

___	H	___	___		___	___	___	___	___	___
368		667	756		991	954	777	667	595	377

Skill: adding three-digit numbers to solve a code

A Quilt Square

Add. Color the spaces with the answers:

Red — Sums less than 400.

White — Sums between 400 and 600.

Blue — Sums greater than 600.

135 + 214	236 + 352	461 + 324	253 + 134
341 + 326	173 + 25 740 + 246	563 + 215 243 + 125	135 + 321
416 + 122	354 + 14 653 + 236	581 + 216 271 + 115	437 + 442
371 + 23	472 + 515	252 + 244	106 + 251

Subtracting Three Numbers

Subtract.	Subtract ones.	Subtract tens.	Subtract hundreds.
365 −242 ———	365 −242 ——— 3	365 −242 ——— 23	365 −242 ——— 123

Subtract.

A.	645 −314	362 −211	958 −737	471 −240
B.	893 −832	685 −110	749 −111	469 −127
C.	647 −204	596 −423	835 −705	578 −132
D.	545 −311	363 −142	450 −250	846 −431

Skill: subtracting three-digit numbers without regrouping

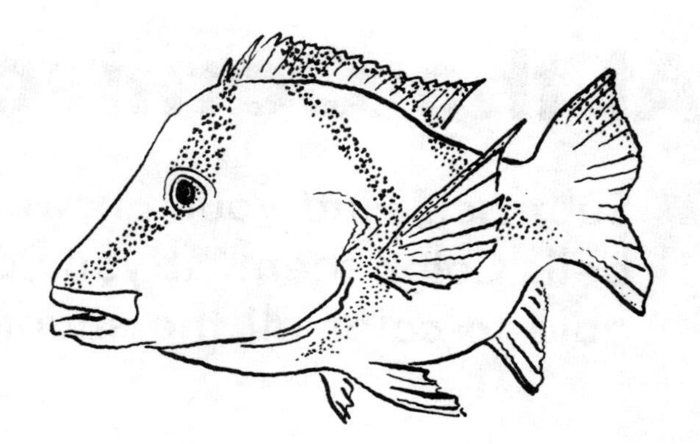

Subtract the ones. Subtract the tens. Then subtract the hundreds.

A.	426 −113	648 −233	759 −537	597 −431
B.	739 −317	436 −120	788 −343	969 −405
C.	568 −101	672 −421	849 −537	733 −423
D.	682 −552	939 −827	665 −234	894 −241

At the Carnival

Subtract. Find your answers on the squares under the bell. Color them. If your answers are correct, you will be able to color all the squares leading to the bell.

9. 627
−412

10. 668
−250

7. 648
−234

8. 659
−234

5. 784
−233

6. 588
−214

3. 658
−221

4. 792
−201

1. 748
−514

2. 567
−132

Skill: subtracting three-digit numbers without regrouping

A Secret Message

Add or subtract. Color in your answers below to find the hidden message.

A.	623 +256	745 −203	38 +421	245 +342	6 +593	477 − 22	123 +860
B.	542 −410	71 +603	298 −174	502 +164	299 − 12	345 +542	564 −221
C.	974 − 21	416 +520	289 −123	846 −312	202 +493	62 +107	599 −301

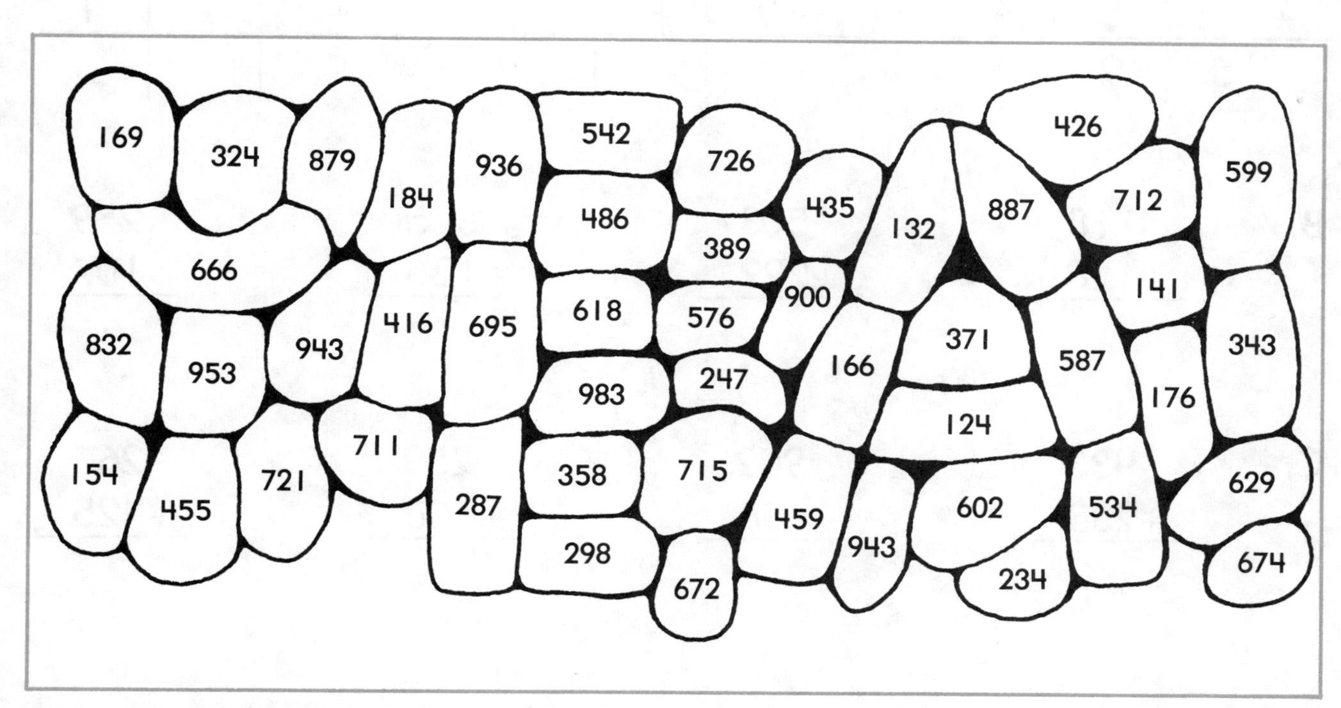

More Regrouping

Add.

365
+427

Add the ones.

hundreds	tens	ones
	1	
3	6	5
+4	2	7
		2

Add the tens.

hundreds	tens	ones
	1	
3	6	5
+4	2	7
	9	2

Add the hundreds.

hundreds	tens	ones
	1	
3	6	5
+ 4	2	7
7	9	2

Add.

1
365
+427
792

Find the sums.

A.

hundreds	tens	ones
	1	
5	3	2
+	5	9
5	9	1

hundreds	tens	ones
2	2	4
+3	4	7

hundreds	tens	ones
1	0	6
+3	7	4

B.

718
+128

503
+229

325
+125

259
+107

C.

433
+238

902
+ 88

259
+106

267
+425

Skill: adding three-digit numbers with regrouping (carrying)

Add. Regroup.

A.

115	324	927	429	356
+236	+247	+ 55	+233	+225

B.

905	463	217	535	268
+ 85	+127	+358	+247	+312

C.

159	248	482	333	136
+126	+445	+109	+319	+ 58

D.

234	509	467	156	784
+617	+ 38	+328	+205	+109

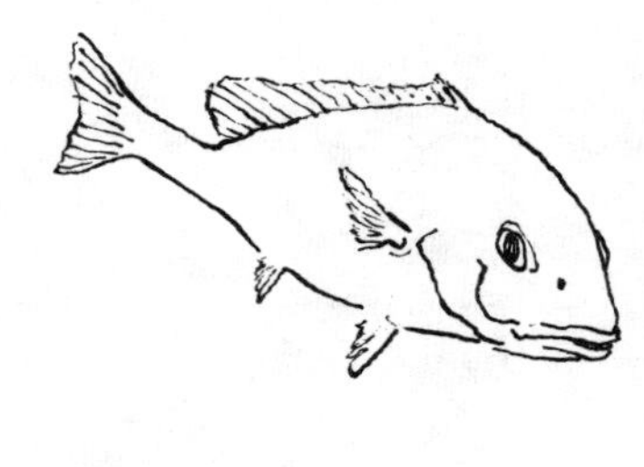

Skill: adding three-digit numbers with regrouping

Add. Regroup.
Match your answers to the number under each line.
Write the letters from the answer boxes on the lines.

A	D	E	G
354 + 218	762 + 128	427 + 343	514 + 149
H	**L**	**M**	**N**
456 + 218	527 + 325	683 + 309	328 + 163
O	**R**	**S**	**T**
728 + 68	156 + 319	946 + 34	328 + 229

What must you know before trying to teach a dog tricks?

M								
992	796	475	770		557	674	572	491

557	674	770		890	796	663

Skill: using addition to complete a code

Who's Hiding?

Add. Color all the spaces with answers greater than 700.

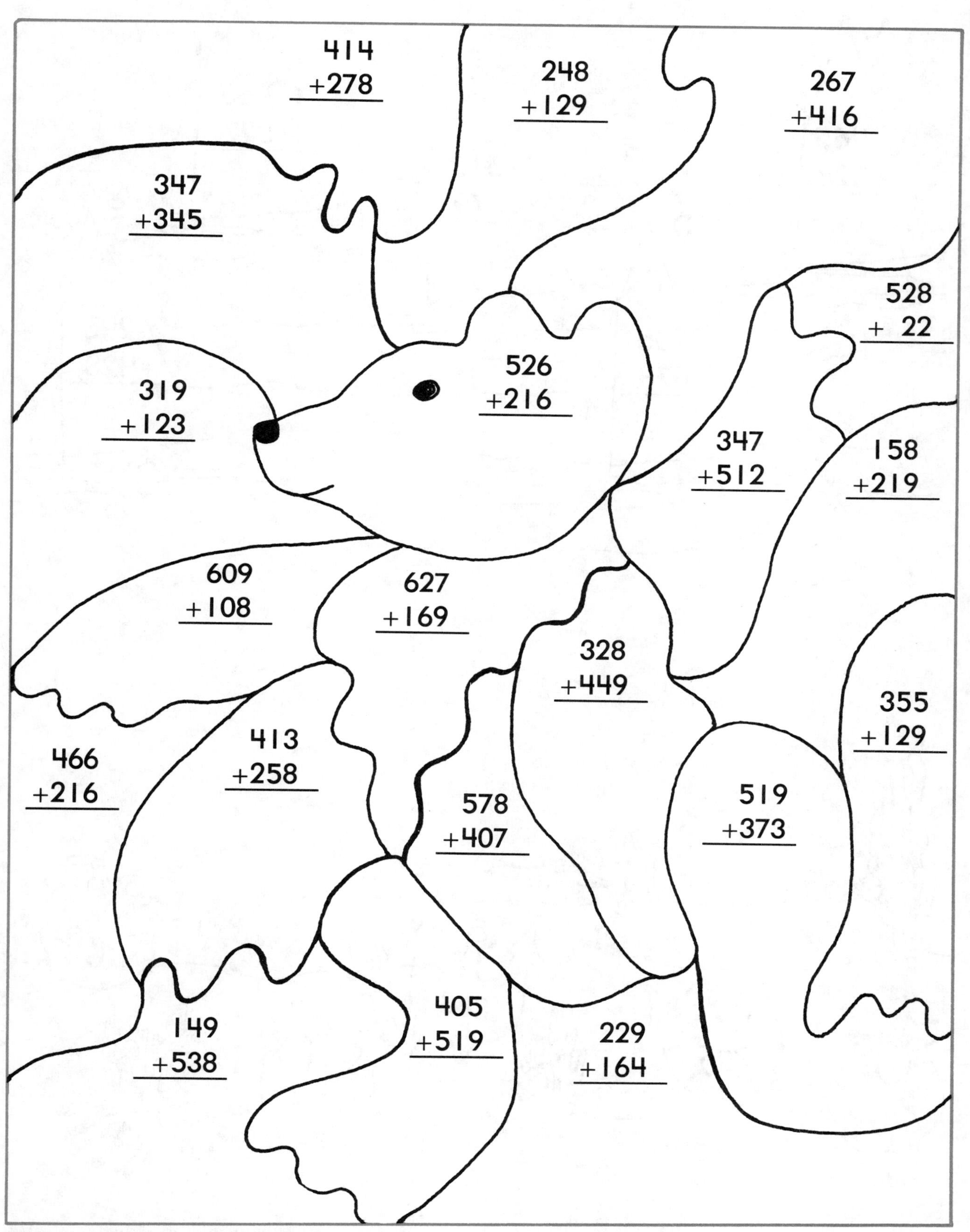

Skill: using addition to complete a hidden picture

Add. Regroup. Find each answer on an anchor. Draw a line from the boat to the matching answer.

Skill: adding three-digit numbers with regrouping

Regrouping with Three Numbers

When you cannot subtract the bottom number from the top number, this is what you must do:

Subtract.

```
 354
-136
```

Regroup.

hundreds	tens	ones
3	~~5~~ 4	~~4~~ 14
−1	3	6

Subtract the ones first.

hundreds	tens	ones
3	~~5~~ 4	~~4~~ 14
−1	3	6
		8

Subtract the tens next.

hundreds	tens	ones
3	~~5~~ 4	~~4~~ 14
−1	3	6
	1	8

Subtract the hundreds.

hundreds	tens	ones
3	~~5~~ 4	~~4~~ 14
−1	3	6
2	1	8

Subtract.

```
  4 14
 3~~5~~~~4~~
-136
 218
```

Subtract.

A.

```
  5 11
 5~~6~~~~1~~     427     635     274
-247    -118    -406    -138
 314
```

B.

```
 625     382     460
-319    - 65    -132
```

C.

```
 276     591     283
-127    -243    -125
```

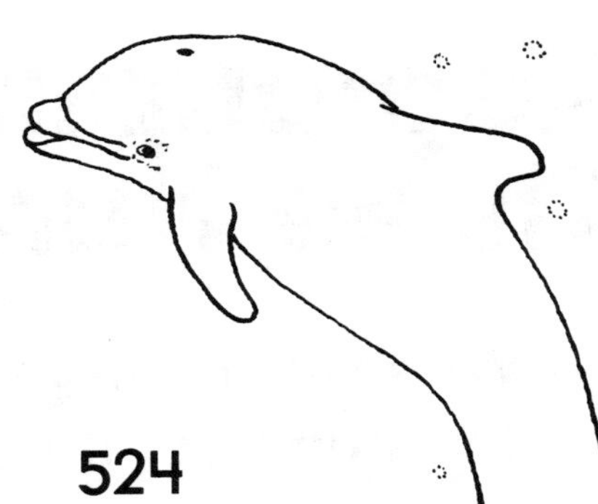

Regroup. Subtract the ones.
Subtract the tens.
Then subtract the hundreds.

A.	$\begin{array}{r} \scriptstyle 2\,11 \\ 6\not{3}\not{1} \\ -519 \\ \hline 112 \end{array}$	$\begin{array}{r} 453 \\ -228 \\ \hline \end{array}$	$\begin{array}{r} 632 \\ -316 \\ \hline \end{array}$	$\begin{array}{r} 524 \\ -107 \\ \hline \end{array}$
B.	$\begin{array}{r} 960 \\ -728 \\ \hline \end{array}$	$\begin{array}{r} 545 \\ -319 \\ \hline \end{array}$	$\begin{array}{r} 674 \\ -569 \\ \hline \end{array}$	$\begin{array}{r} 587 \\ -148 \\ \hline \end{array}$
C.	$\begin{array}{r} 892 \\ -375 \\ \hline \end{array}$	$\begin{array}{r} 296 \\ -168 \\ \hline \end{array}$	$\begin{array}{r} 963 \\ -118 \\ \hline \end{array}$	$\begin{array}{r} 571 \\ -139 \\ \hline \end{array}$
D.	$\begin{array}{r} 733 \\ -626 \\ \hline \end{array}$	$\begin{array}{r} 626 \\ -107 \\ \hline \end{array}$	$\begin{array}{r} 335 \\ -217 \\ \hline \end{array}$	$\begin{array}{r} 462 \\ -143 \\ \hline \end{array}$

Skill: subtracting three-digit numbers with regrouping

Regroup.
Subtract. Color the rocks with answers less than 200 to see where the frog jumped.

An Elephant Riddle

Regroup. Subtract.
Match your answers to the number under each line. Write the letters from the answer boxes on the lines.

A	C	E	H
596 − 107	661 − 34	540 − 201	656 − 338
I	**K**	**N**	**P**
590 − 186	383 − 135	185 − 76	452 − 233
R	**T**	**U**	**Y**
681 − 442	620 − 211	860 − 531	274 − 39

Why were the elephants the last to leave the ark?

T (409) ___ (318) ___ (339) ___ (235)   ___ (318) ___ (489) D   ___ (409) O

___ (219) ___ (489) ___ (627) ___ (248)   ___ (409) ___ (318) ___ (339) ___ (404) ___ (239)

___ (409) ___ (239) ___ (329) ___ (109) ___ (248) S !

Skill: using subtraction to complete a code

Find the Pattern

Regroup. Subtract.
Color the spaces with the answers:

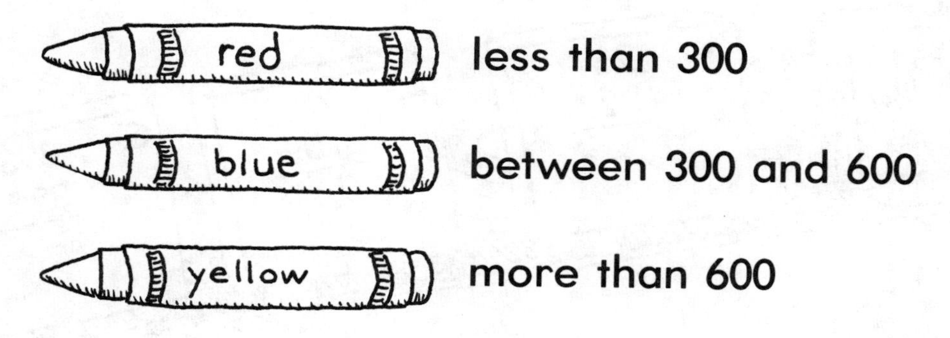

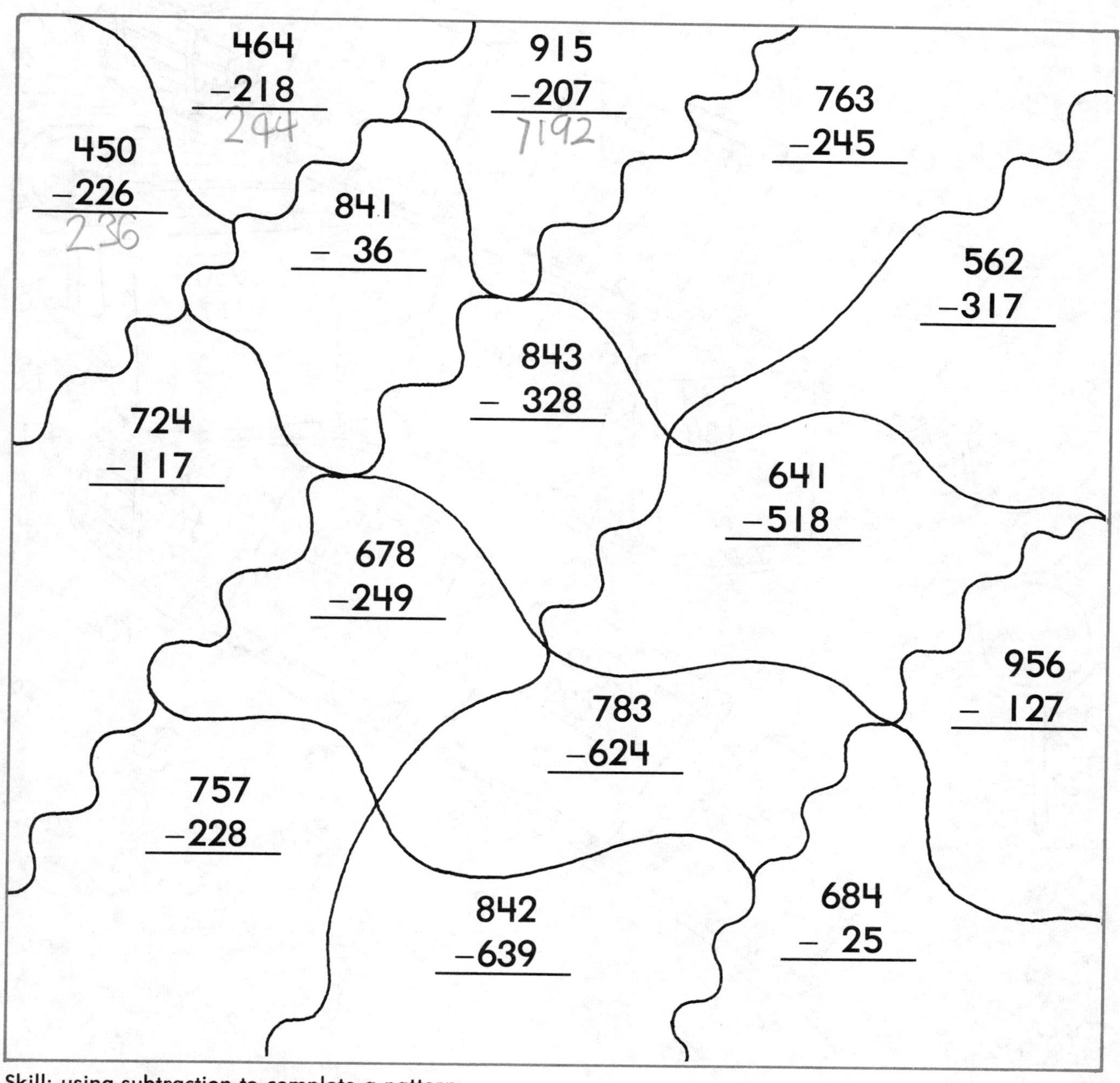

Add or subtract.
Regroup.
Watch the signs.
A. 257 +323
B. 781 −109
C. 893 −329
D. 175 +115
E. 357 +517
F. 891 −458
G. 354 +138
H. 175 +206
I. 980 −717
J. 581 −138
K. 642 +229
L. 394 −128

Election Time

Votes for Mayor

	Mr. Barry	Mrs. Kane	Mr. Turner
Men	432	233	326
Women	143	422	318

Use the chart to answer the questions. Add or subtract.

	Work here.		Work here.
1. How many men voted in all?	432 233 +326	5. How many more men voted for Mr. Turner than women?	
2. How many women voted in all?		6. How many votes did Mr. Barry get in all?	
3. How many more men voted than women? (Hint: use your answers in 1 and 2.)		7. How many votes did Mrs. Kane get in all?	
		8. How many votes did Mr. Turner get in all?	
4. How many more women voted for Mrs. Kane than Mr. Turner?		9. Who won the election? ________________	

Skills: reading a table; using addition and subtraction to solve word problems

A Day at the Zoo

Add or subtract to solve the word problems.

	Work here.
1. 327 people visited the zoo on Saturday. On Sunday 455 people came to the zoo. How many more people visited the zoo on Sunday?	455 −327
2. The elephants at the zoo eat 246 pounds of feed in the morning and 318 pounds at night. How many pounds of feed do they eat in a day?	
3. The zoo has 126 American songbirds in a big room. In a larger room the zoo has 474 tropical birds. How many more tropical birds does the zoo have?	
4. In one week the zoo sold 443 boxes of popcorn. The next week the zoo sold 529 boxes. How many boxes of popcorn did the zoo sell in two weeks?	
5. The zoo has a train ride and a cable car ride. On Saturday 148 people rode the train. 129 people rode the cable car. How many more people rode the train?	

Skill: using addition and subtraction to solve word problems

The Weight Room

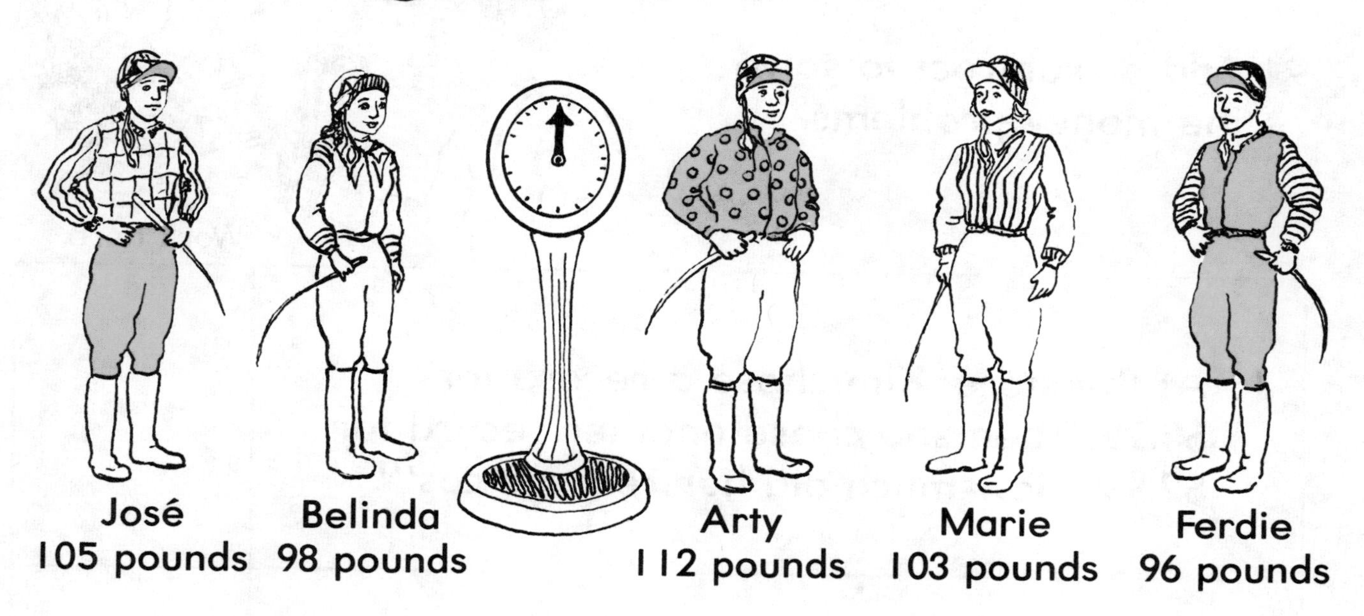

Add or subtract to solve the problems.

	Work here.		Work here.
1. How much more does Marie weigh than Ferdie?		4. Arty is supposed to weigh in at 109 pounds. How much weight must he lose?	
2. José's equipment weighs 37 pounds. How much does José and his equipment weigh in all?		5. How much do Arty and José weigh together?	
3. Ferdie can weigh up to 105 pounds. How much more can he weigh?		6. Belinda has to weigh 126 pounds to race. How much extra weight will she have to carry?	

Skill: using addition and subtraction to solve word problems

At the Store

Add or subtract to solve the money problems.

	Work here.
1. At the store, Kim chose a record for \$3.29. Then she chose another record for \$2.49. How much did her records cost?	
2. Bill had \$1.60. He bought a magazine for \$1.15. How much money did he have left?	
3. Carmen bought a package of gum for 49¢ and a paperback book for \$1.50. How much did she spend?	
4. Ginny bought a package of stickers for 78¢. She bought a pencil for 29¢. How much more did the stickers cost than the pencil?	
5. Matt bought a package of markers for \$1.25, a box of candy for 35¢, and a baseball cap for \$6.27. How much did he spend in all?	

Skill: using money to solve word problems

ANSWERS

Page 1
A. 4, 7, 8, 7, 9
B. 6, 9, 12, 10, 12
C. 15, 14, 13, 8, 11
D. 10, 17, 15, 18, 13
E. 11, 12, 14, 13, 16

Page 2
A. 11, 10, 8
B. 12, 10, 5
C. 4, 12, 9
D. 7, 9, 6
E. 13, 12, 8
F. 9, 11, 14
G. 10, 7, 12
H. 17, 14, 15
I. 11, 16, 13

Page 3

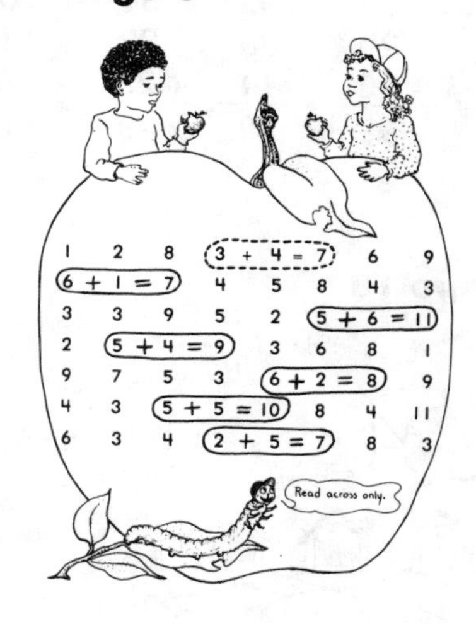

Page 4

2	2	4
3	4	7
5	6	11

A.

3	2	5
1	4	5
4	6	10

B.

1	4	5
3	1	4
4	5	9

C.

3	1	4
1	3	4
4	4	8

D.

5	1	6
1	4	5
6	5	11

E.

1	2	3
3	4	7
4	6	10

F.

3	3	6
1	2	3
4	5	9

G.

5	2	7
2	5	7
7	7	14

H.

3	5	8
2	2	4
5	7	12

Page 5
A. 3, 7, 3, 2, 4
B. 3, 6, 3, 8, 9
C. 6, 8, 5, 4, 9

Page 6
A. 18, 13, 15, 12, 16, 11
B. 9, 10, 17, 17, 14, 12
C. 4, 1, 4, 7, 7, 8

Page 7
A. 4, 3, 0
B. 1, 4, 6, 9, 7
C. 6, 5, 9
D. 6, 8, 7, 3, 9
E. 5, 8, 9
F. 4, 7, 8, 4, 6

Page 8
A. 1, 4, 7, 8
B. 6, 2, 5
C. 7, 0, 5, 3
Wish on a Star

Page 9

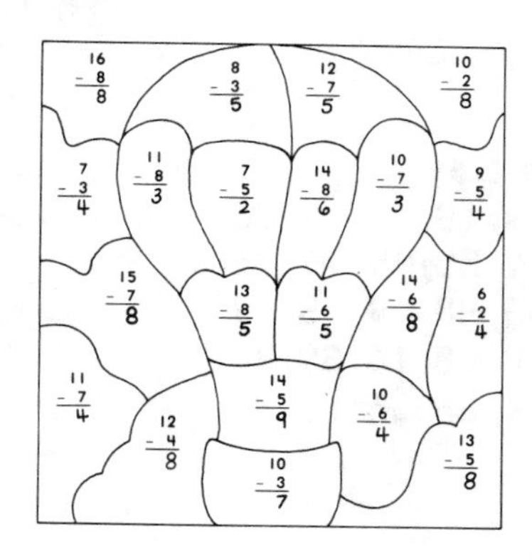

Page 10
A. 14, 6, 11, 9, 8
B. 7, 7, 18, 11, 3
C. 5, 10, 6, 15, 9
D. 16, 8, 12, 3, 13

Page 11
A. 8, 7, 10
B. 16, 13, 6
C. 2, 8, 11
D. 9, 13, 17
E. 6, 8, 15
F. +, −
G. +, −

Page 12
A. 44, 49, 97, 78
B. 18, 48, 54, 49
C. 59, 89, 52, 66

Page 13
A. 64, 49, 65
B. 86, 77, 58, 69, 94
C. 99, 78, 93, 68, 55
D. 78, 86, 97, 48, 59
E. 65, 99

Page 14

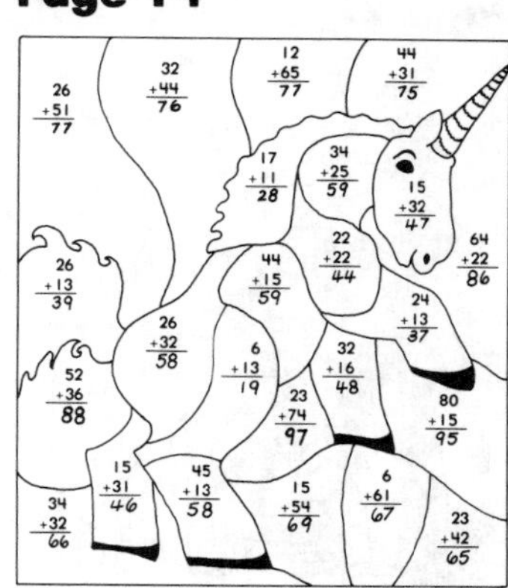

Page 15
A. 99, 98, 87, 97
B. 58, 79, 89, 63
C.

62	42	31	70
24	36	22	11
+ 13	+ 11	+ 25	+ 16
99	89	78	97

Page 16
A. 22, 41, 24, 12
B. 36, 13, 33, 70
C. 17, 42, 15, 13

Page 17
A. 45, 24, 11
B. 30, 41, 22, 35, 41
C. 50, 62, 24, 13, 31
D. 52, 36, 64, 63, 55
E. 32, 46

Page 18

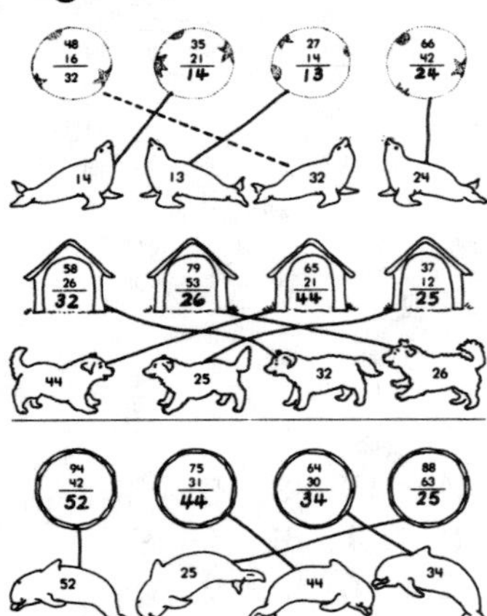

Page 19
A. 38, 53, 89, 48, 88
B. 34, 67, 62, 49, 23
C. 66, 33, 57, 64, 68

Page 20
A. 62, 68, 57, 22, 98
B. 46, 40, 78, 66, 5
C. 39, 88, 53, 16, 89
D. 31, 99, 10, 79, 25

Page 21
A. 84, 41, 85, 71, 83
B. 91, 81, 80, 91, 74
C. 43, 62, 91, 83, 94

Page 22
A. 48, 94, 51, 70
B. 42, 43, 71, 61, 93
C. 51, 72, 90, 52, 74
D. 75, 76, 61, 74, 96

Page 23
A. 81, 82, 57, 63, 75
B. 44, 90, 83, 93, 86
C. 35, 70, 72, 55, 80
D. 66, 60, 82, 94, 81

Page 24
A. 39, 15, 7, 16, 15
B. 49, 25, 17, 58, 66

Page 25
A. 19, 18, 28, 39, 26
B. 12, 55, 45, 79, 25
C. 13, 48, 9, 8, 19
D. 18, 8, 16, 39, 48
E. 19, 38, 6, 15, 37

Page 26

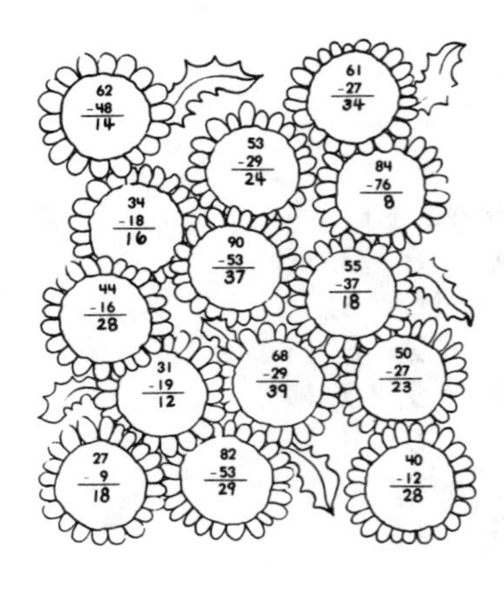

Page 27

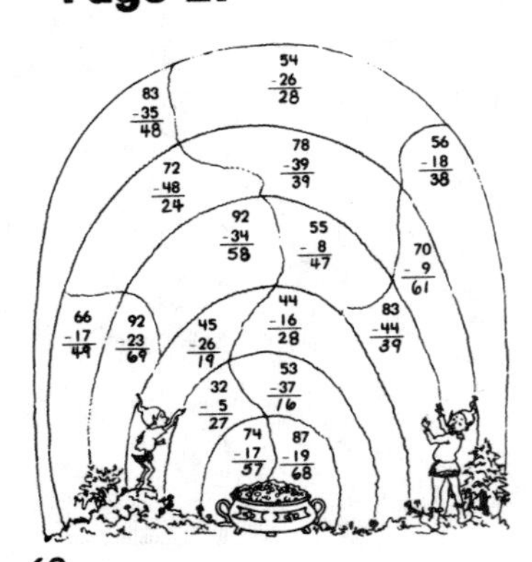

Page 28
A. 47, 71, 95, 19, 3
B. 91, 64, 13, 82, 46
C. 32, 94, 80, 28, 33
D. 75, 80, 49, 35, 83

Page 29
90, 59, 60, 65, 71
28, 83, 39, 51, 34
63, 91, 36, 81, 17
To Keep Their Sunglasses Dry

Page 30

A. 90 − 8 = 82	B. 24 + 72 = 96	C. 72 − 28 = 44	D. 50 − 7 = 43	E. 62 + 29 = 91	F. 94 − 17 = 77
G. 15 + 75 = 90	H. 49 + 31 = 80	I. 46 + 46 = 92	J. 80 − 9 = 71	K. 82 − 16 = 66	L. 91 − 18 = 73
M. 45 + 25 = 70	N. 36 + 45 = 81	O. 71 − 29 = 42	P. 24 + 29 = 53	Q. 66 + 35 = 101	R. 90 − 49 = 41

START → 82 … FINISH

Page 31

A. 15 B. 17
C. 2 D. 3
E. 14 F. 9

Page 32

A. 17 B. 59
C. 51 D. 35

Page 33

A. 8 B. 61
C. 73 D. 81
E. 8

Page 34

A. 95 B. 22
C. 17 D. 55

Page 35

A. 326, 584, 615
B. 4 hundreds 7 tens 2 ones
9 hundreds 2 tens 6 ones
1 hundred 5 tens 3 ones
C. 438, 620, 305
D. 8 hundreds 5 tens 0 ones
4 hundreds 0 tens 7 ones

Page 36

	hundreds	tens	ones
A.	1	3	5
B.	2	5	1
C.	1	4	4
D.	4	2	6
E.	3	1	8
F.	2	2	3

Page 38

2	1	8	■	3	7	7
1	6	2	■	4	3	1
■	■	5	7	0	■	■
1	5	■	6	■	9	8
■	■	3	6	4	■	■
5	2	7	■	1	4	9
7	0	6	■	3	2	1

Page 39

A. 836, 678, 795, 586
B. 559, 798, 899, 647
C. 796, 598, 789, 488
D. 579, 667, 564, 549

Page 40

595, 496, 859, 667
999, 377, 766, 954
991, 368, 777, 756
Mice, Because They Squeak

Page 41

135 + 214 = 349; 236 + 352 = 588; 461 + 324 = 785; 253 + 134 = 387
341 + 326 = 667; 173 + 25 = 198; 563 + 215 = 778; 135 + 321 = 456
740 + 246 = 986; 243 + 125 = 368
416 + 122 = 538; 354 + 14 = 368; 581 + 216 = 797; 437 + 442 = 879
653 + 236 = 889; 271 + 115 = 386
371 + 23 = 394; 472 + 515 = 987; 252 + 244 = 496; 106 + 251 = 357

Page 42

A. 331, 151, 221, 231
B. 61, 575, 638, 342
C. 443, 173, 130, 446
D. 234, 221, 200, 415

Page 43

A. 313, 415, 222, 166
B. 422, 316, 445, 564
C. 467, 251, 312, 310
D. 130, 112, 431, 653

Page 44

1. 234 2. 435
3. 437 4. 591
5. 551 6. 374
7. 414 8. 425
9. 215 10. 418

Page 45

A. 879, 542, 459, 587, 599, 455, 983
B. 132, 674, 124, 666, 287, 887, 343
C. 953, 936, 166, 534, 695, 169, 298
YEA!

Page 46

A. 591, 571, 480,
B. 846, 732, 450, 366
C. 671, 990, 365, 692

Page 47

A. 351, 571, 982, 662, 581
B. 990, 590, 575, 782, 580
C. 285, 693, 591, 652, 194
D. 851, 547, 795, 361, 893

Page 48

572, 890, 770, 663
674, 852, 992, 491
796, 475, 980, 557
More Than The Dog

Page 49

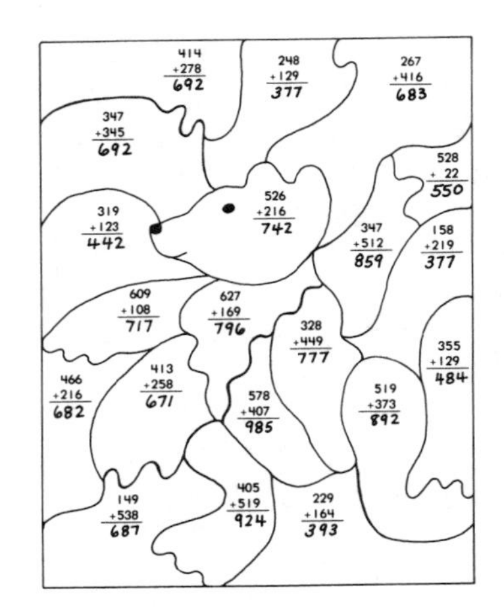

Page 50

A. 793 B. 692
C. 790 D. 883
E. 674

Page 51

A. 314, 309, 229, 136
B. 306, 317, 328
C. 149, 348, 158

Page 52

A. 112, 225, 316, 417
B. 232, 226, 105, 439
C. 517, 128, 845, 432
D. 107, 519, 118, 319

Page 53

Page 54

489, 627, 339, 318
404, 248, 109, 219
239, 409, 329, 235
They Had to Pack Their Trunks!

Page 55

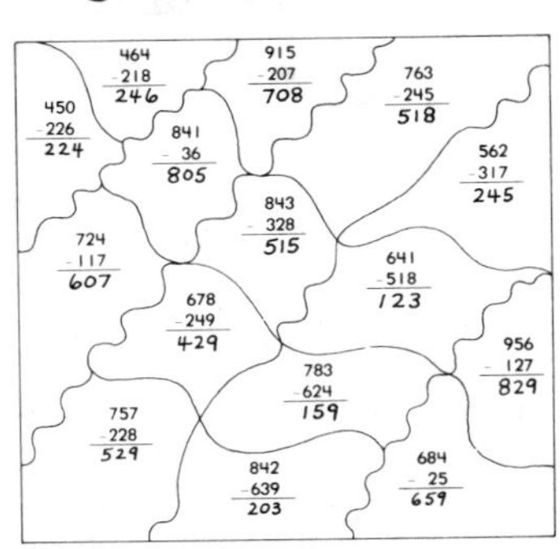

Page 56

A. 580 B. 672
C. 564 D. 290
E. 874 F. 433
G. 492 H. 381
I. 263 J. 443
K. 871 L. 266

Page 57

1. 991 2. 883
3. 108 4. 104
5. 8 6. 575
7. 655 8. 644
9. Mrs. Kane

Page 58

1. 128 2. 564
3. 348 4. 972
5. 19

Page 59

1. 7 pounds
2. 142 pounds
3. 9 pounds
4. 3 pounds
5. 217 pounds
6. 28 pounds

Page 60

1. $5.78
2. $ .45
3. $1.99
4. 49¢
5. $7.87